The 7th Day

with the short story "Devil Dog"

by Frederick Faust, writing as

MAX BRAND

Illustrated by

Charles LaSalle

Harold Wellington McCrea

ADELAIDE & SHEPPARD

Introduction

BY ANDREW SALMON

WHENEVER WESTERN fiction is discussed, three names are always mentioned ahead of the rest: Zane Grey, Louis L'Amour, and Max Brand. Frederick Faust (aka Max Brand) will always be known as one of the greatest Western writers in the history of the genre and with good reason because he excelled at them. He gave us hundreds of memorable tales and a host of characters from Speedy to Silvertip, Dan Barry and Destry. His stories from the "mountain desert" are timeless in theme, language, characterization and evocative imagery.

But to limit him to one genre does him a disservice. Faust, like any pulp writer worth his or her salt, wrote in numerous genres for the vast pulp market of the time. Yet today, he's pigeon-holed as a Western author and any reader encountering his work for the first time will most likely come to it via an interest in Westerns. That's okay because, I repeat, Faust was one of the all-time best.

One of the all-time best fiction writers, that is. Period. However his work does not often get a chance to display its versatility these days. In the 74 years since Faust, working as a war correspondent for *Harper's Magazine,* was killed in action in the WWII battle of Santa Maria Infante in May, 1944, publishers have provided a steady stream of his Westerns for the reading public. This made sense at first as the Western ruled the big screen and newsstands back then and, eventually, the TV screen as well in the years following Faust's untimely demise. As a result, a mountain of non-Western material he created for the pulps has been consigned to the crumbling pages of old pulp magazines and yellowing slicks. Even today, there are a handful of publishers regularly re-issuing his Western tales but not enough attention is being paid to his other work. Faust wrote detective, mystery, sports, science-fiction, pirate, high seas adventure and spy tales as readily as he crafted tales of blazing six-guns. He created Dr. Kildare and guided the young doctor through eight novels while his exploits played across the silver screen. Though not as numerous as his Western fiction, many of these are well worth the time of today's readers.

And now, *The 7th Day*. This seven-part serial ran in *Maclean's Magazine* from January 1–April 1, 1938. The novel is one of three appearances Faust made in the Canadian magazine, the others being another novel, *A Seabold Fights* (November 15, 1936–February 15, 1937), and a short story, "Devil Dog" (June 15, 1938), which rounds out this volume.

In *The 7th Day* we are introduced to Tony Newcomen, a fiction writer living in Venice when his friend, mentor and business manager, Thomas Decker, calls him to Florence amidst the lavish estates and is murdered while Newcomen is talking to him on the phone. What follows is a character-driven drama that Faust did not have to stretch to far to envision.

Faust, a pulp writer, had been living in a lavish villa in Florence for the previous ten years. Earning the top word rate for his incredible output of fiction for so long, Faust could afford to live more like a Roman Governor than a producer of purple prose. And this was during the Depression don't forget. Sprawling grounds, a large swimming pool, tennis court—the works! There's a reason Faust was called "the King of the Pulps" during his lifetime. Faust sold almost 30,000,000 words to the pulps and slicks in 27 years as a professional writers. He made and spent fortunes annually to support his lifestyle and his generosity made him a very soft touch. His willingness to help the down and out no doubt sprang from his desperate younger years of knocking around the country and going through the starving artist phase all creators must go through. His was particularly rough with far too many lean days and years which left so deep a mark he could not stand to see anyone else go through hard times. Sadly as a result, he was always a few sales away from being back in that position. In the meantime, he lived large and money was merely a means to that end.

His friends and family said later that Florence was where Faust seemed the most at home and he hated to leave when the rise of fascism in Italy and Germany drove him back to the United States in 1938 where he, reluctantly, settled into a Hollywood writing job at MGM for a steady $1,250 a week. With some of his pulp and slick markets beginning to dry up and his word rate having been cut forcing him to leave his prime source of income, *Western Story Magazine*, this was an attempt to stem the tide of expenses and debts his continual influx of money from magazine sales and book royalties couldn't quite conquer. Launching the Dr. Kildare series in Hollywood added to coffers that badly needed filling.

As readers, we can trust Faust's depiction of Florence in *The 7th Day*. He lived it, he loved it and this shines through with his spot-on characterizations and evocative descriptions. The novel is not hardboiled fare. Faust knew the market he was writing for and the characters owe more to the drawing room of Agatha Christie than the back alleys of Dashiell Hammett with a melodramatic love affair more suited to Shakespeare, whom Faust adored, added to the plot. That's not to say there is no action in the tale. There are a handful of action sequences which will not disappoint while the whodunit plot will keep you turning pages as we learn more and more about the suspects. Faust even throws a huge dog into the mix to keep thing interesting and be a central point to the plot halfway through the novel.

Newcomen seems a little out of place at times amongst the idle rich high society setting. He plays his cards close to the vest throughout the tale. He bribes one of the female suspects to stay in Florence for seven days (thus the title), not only because he's instantly smitten with her but because he thinks she may have murdered his friend and wants to keep her around if he can prove her guilt. He seems to relish toying with the suspects and placing himself in danger in his determination to unmask Decker's killer at any cost. He manages to be single-minded in this without coming across as hardboiled.

The novel is also well-paced. With its leaning towards melodrama, one might expect long drawn out sequences of interior monologue and gothic descriptions of settings and so on as we find in Faust's densely psychological dramas like *The Garden of Eden* or *Monsieur*. But in *The 7th Day,* Faust tells the story mostly through dialogue. He had a great ear for language and, by having the characters reveal themselves more through words than actions, the plot is stripped down for easy digestion and the pace remains brisk. The action sequences erupt as a result in their suddenness. Faust knew how to deliver an engaging reading experience and he does that with *The 7th Day.*

Also included with the novel is "Devil Dog," a short story that is an animal lover's dream. Here we follow Samuel Cornwall Gresham, a free spirited man who is in Alaska digging gold to pay his way through medical school. He's quite content minding his own business in the frozen wastes when the monster-like Jarvis barges into Gresham's cabin and has his huge dog, Chris, viciously kill Gresham's two smaller animals before helping himself to food and, upon leaving, Gresham's stash of gold dust he'd amass through back-breaking work.

A rousing chase across the frozen wastes ensues as Jarvis tries to elude Gresham and the men the would-be doctor enlisted to help with the hunt while the dog, Chris, is hot on the heels of his master. The story is an all-out action yarn with great pacing and room for a lot of heart as well. You'll feel the biting cold and stinging wind as you chase along with Gresham and crew. To reveal more would be to spoil the fun but the story poses the question of what is more valuable: gold dust or friendship. It's a great read that has been waiting for a new audience these last eighty years. It's tailor made for today's reader.

I've only been reading the work of Frederick Faust for about a dozen years now and what amazes me as I look over my bookshelves, is that I've already read more than 100 of his books in that short period of time. And I have more than that number to look forward to with more coming out every year. It's a testament to his talent that, in only a handful of years, I have read more of his work than any other author I've read in my lifetime. And I've been a voracious reader all my life. That's partly due to the mountain of work he produced but also, and more importantly, his voice keeps me coming back for more. Just as he seemed insatiable in the amount of work he strove to produce, I, and generations of readers before me, keep coming back to sample more of his stuff. Which is why it's so important to have the full range of his talent available for us to enjoy.

One of the great surprises is picking up a Max Brand book—or any of the other eighteen pen-names Frederick Faust used—without any foreknowledge of the material. He wrote so well and in so many genres and styles that cold starting any of his tales is tremendously exciting. You just never know what you're going to get. You know it will be well-written in all aspects of the game. But will it be an all-out actioner, an introspective character study, a psychological exploration of a human being and his or her place in the world, a simple good versus evil plot or a blurring of those opposing forces? A master storyteller sweeps you up and carries you along for the ride. Faust was one of the best ever at pulling this off and it's not as easy as it looks, believe me.

So sit back and let *The 7th Day* and "Devil Dog" unfold. You're in the hands of one of the best storytellers who ever lived. Enjoy the ride!

The 7th Day

"FEAR," SAID the voice over the telephone. "I mean that, Tony. I'm sitting here in my own study and I can smell murder. As clearly as you ever smelled mildew in a damp cellar. Get out of Venice and come to me; now; tonight."

Anthony Newcomen, newly wakened by the snoring buzzer of the telephone beside his bed, turned on his side and looked out the hotel window at the illumined face of Santa Maria della Salute across the Grand Canal. San Giorgio retired obscurely to the left, and from the anchored barge off the Custom House the musicians kept weaving a tarnished thread of *fiesta* even this far into the night.

"Hello, Tony! Are you hearing me? Are you hearing me?" insisted the voice.

"I'm hearing you, Tom," said Newcomen. He was seeing Thomas Decker, too, the middle-aged joviality with a touch of grey fox. That picture always had prevented him from accepting Decker as a second father.

"You don't believe me; you think it's nerves?" said Decker.

"Tom, you're not serious about being afraid of your own shadow, in your own house?"

"I'm sick with fear, Tony. It's like dust up my nose. I can't breathe."

"I'll drive over tomorrow afternoon."

"No, come now. Will you come now?"

"Take a good shot of brandy and go to bed," said Newcomen.

"Tony, is there anything womanish about me?"

Newcomen remembered for a moment the hard, cold alertness of those eyes. "No. You're not a nervous type," he said.

"I'm going to risk telling you over the telephone," said Decker, lowering his voice. "Can you hear me?"

"I smell murder...
I'm sick with fear...
Come now... I can't
risk telling...."

The voice sounded faintly above the windy murmurings that ran over the wire.

"I can hear you, barely. What are you going to tell me?" asked Newcomen.

"I'm telling you that I saw murder in a face today."

"What are you talking about? Murder?"

"You never saw it or I wouldn't have to describe it. Cat's eyes, and a wolf's grin... It's a horrible thing and I saw it today. My flesh crawls on my bones when I think of it."

"It sounds like a nightmare," said Newcomen.

"It is. A nightmare, with your eyes open, and your heart falling as though you were in a dream."

"I'm starting now. I'll come as fast as a motor will bring me. But tell me the name."

"I can't risk it."

"I've got to know. Tell me who it is."

"Shall I?" said Thomas Decker. "Yes, I will. The name is..."

The voice of Thomas Decker, which had fallen away to a half-heard murmuring, sounded again loudly in a wordless cry; the telephone clicked; only the monotonous, empty humming lived in the ear of Newcomen.

HE WAITED, incredulous, his eye wandering automatically about the room from the gilded pilasters that framed the great mirror to the chandelier whose crystals never quite stopped jangling day or night, telling him that he was not still in New York dreaming out a crime-story plot but actually in Venice, the well beloved, with only the Apennines between him and his Florence. And from the famous hillside which overlooks Florence his old friend and financial agent, Thomas Decker, had just slammed up his telephone on a cry that was either pain or fear.

The line was dead now. Newcomen got the *concierge* of his

place and said: "Call Florence. I want to speak to Thomas Decker at his villa in San Domenico. Rush it."

He got out of bed and stood on the dampness of the rug, pulling clothes over his big body with unthinking hands, for his mind was over there on the other side of the mountains, running through the evergreen gardens of the Decker place, learning tennis again inside the dark cypress hedges of its court, learning to dive and swim in its colonnaded pool, walking again through the shadowy vastness of the rooms, smelling once more the bindings in the library, or falling asleep in front of one of the lofty fireplaces with the sweetness of burning pine cones still in the air. Since the death of his father, Newcomen had spent half his life in the care of Decker.

The telephone rang. He snatched it up.

"The Florence operator says that there is no answer from Mr. Decker," said the *concierge*.

"There has to be an answer; I was talking to Mr. Decker only a few minutes ago and...."

Here his voice stopped in his throat.

He added: "Get my bill ready, please. Call the garage. Tell them to check my car for gas and oil. Call a motor launch. I'm leaving at once."

The launch carried him swiftly up the Grand Canal, shouldering before it two sleek waves of moonlight. He saw them curl out to the feet of the old palaces, half of them with their eyes blinded by shutters, their faces too delicate to withstand time.

The wide flat arch of the Rialto bridge pressed a black hand across his eyes. Then all his thoughts were far off in San Domenico until he found his car singing over the long bridge to the mainland with the moist air whipping his face cold, for he had the top of the convertible back. From the end of the bridge the road turned sharply left. He got to eighty, to ninety over the straight of it. He touched a hundred. The flicking of his hair stung his forehead at that speed. Then he was looping along the river road with the old villas shuffling away like picture cards behind him. Only when he straightened away for Padua, the dampness left the air and the dry acrid smell of summer dust took its place. To the horizon, vineyards glimmered under the moonlight; then he entered the gate of Padua and ran into ovenlike warmth, still husbanded from the day in the narrow streets.

Clouds shut him from the moon. Rain had been falling on the heights. It came again in thick gusts. Then the rainclouds themselves poured in around him. The headlights vainly struck at the white mist. He drove by guess and glimpses of the wet road, while all its curves came gradually back into the forgotten chart of his mind.

The dawn came up while he still was on the heights; and at last he saw Florence, dark in its great hollow among the hills though the morning already floated a skyful of big cumulus clouds in a rosy brilliance. He let that famous picture of towers and domes slip unnoticed through his eyes. What he wanted was Decker's Villa Oliviera, and up the narrow ways of San Domenico the whine of the motor grew loud with the echoes between the high walls.

IT WAS too early for the people to be up in the gardener's cottage, so he did not stop to blow his horn or jangle the bell at the locked entrance gate. He went straight by it, and halted the car by the big stone wall that gave privacy from the highway. Newcomen went over that wall with the ease of long practice, for he had used the short cut when he was a boy, paying visits to the *villino* which was part of the estate though it lay across the public road.

He dropped from the wall upon the lowest terrace of the garden. The tennis court was on his left, but all the levels were named from the sculpture that ornamented them. This was the Diana Terrace, for instance, named after a good figure of the huntress as

"You mustn't steal my reputation," said Dinah Moore.

"I want to buy it," said Anthony. "Say, for a thousand dollars."

she was about to whip an arrow out of the quiver; unfortunately her face had been reduced to a smiling blur by the centuries.

Newcomen ran up steps paved with a mosaic of colored pebbles to the Dancers' Terrace above, named for a group of dancing street gamins which an eighteenth century sculptor had carved with great abandon. Here a sort of Philosopher's Walk extended through a gloom of ancient cypresses. He reached the level which took its name from a huge smiling Hercules who leaned on his club, half lost in the surrounding greenery. Grass was gone from a small patch, and in the mud which the rain of the night before had made, Newcomen saw clearly the print of the forefoot of a big dog, with one claw missing. He saw the imprint distinctly, just before his descending foot involuntarily struck the place and blotted out the sign completely.

Five minutes later he came down again over the same terraces more quickly, his head turning continually to look behind. When he reached the boundary wall, he looked from the top of it, earnestly, up and down the bend of the road. It lay empty beneath him, but a fine dust, like morning mist, hung between the walls that fenced the road and proved that some vehicle had passed not long before. His car had been seen, therefore. That thought pinched his lips together before he swung over the wall and dropped to the road.

After that, he drove on to the iron entrance gates and honked to have them opened. Old Angelina, the gardener's wife, came out, shielding her eyes from the morning sun, and swung the heavy panels wide. He stopped the car when it was halfway in, calling: "Angelina! Bad women have bad eyes! Or have you forgotten me?"

She threw up both arms and left them on high, frozen with delight, and crying out: "*Il signorino! O caro! O ben ritornato!*"

She was so old that joy made her cry. She was so happy that she tried to kiss his hand, but he took it away from her and patted her shoulder. She had only one tooth in front.

Old Beppo appeared at that moment, running over the grass on legs stilted by age. He came with a distracted face, held out a hand before him as though he were in a hurry to give away his bad news.

"Angelina, misery has come on us!" he cried. "The *signore* is dead. On the Hercules Terrace. He is lying dead by the pond of water lilies. Tell me what we can do?"

He saw Newcomen then and groaned out: "Ah, *signorino,* God has sent you to help us in trouble. The *signore* is dead! He is dead on the Hercules Terrace!"

HUGH CHURCHILL, as secretary for so many years to rich Thomas Decker and an intimate counsellor in most of his affairs, constantly expected to be treated as something more than a domestic servant and was constantly disappointed; for Decker was fond of saying that servants are great conveniences until they become masters. As a result, after fifteen years of service Churchill found himself housed in a north room whose walls were not big enough to hang his pictures, for like his master he was a collector.

A northern exposure, darkened by a row of big cypresses just outside his window, left his room in a dingy twilight except toward the middle of the day. On this morning he wakened with a start and peered earnestly around him, but found everything as tarnished and dim as the figures in some rain-washed fresco of the Quatrocento. Yet he knew that someone was in the room with him. He could feel the unseen eye like an inward sense of guilt; and he wondered if clever thieves had realized that that

Madonna and Child might be—God willing—a Romano? He got as far as this in his thoughts and was reaching stealthily for his glasses on the bedside table, when the deep voice of a man spoke out of the stains and shadows of the room: "Don't be alarmed, Churchill. It's Tony."

"The *signorino!*" exclaimed Churchill. "I beg your pardon, Mr. Newcomen—old habits of speech, Tony."

He got up from the bed while he was talking. Now, with the glasses settled on his nose, he could make out the dimensions of Anthony with his usual surprise. For years he had tried to look down at Newcomen and always found himself looking up instead. The boy had vanished too suddenly and left a man in his place before Churchill could get used to the change. It was not only that Newcomen was tall and broad but he gave to people a sense of still greater bigness, a thing which sometimes comes to pass when mind is mixed with matter in the way which artists know, or ought to know.

"You're already dressed," observed Newcomen.

"Dressed?" said Churchill. He looked down at his clothes and seemed to discover them with surprise. "Yes, yes. Dressed. Got up for a breath of early air."

"You must do some telephoning," directed Newcomen. "You'll know what police official to reach. Mr. Decker is dead."

"Is what? Is what?" cried out Churchill. He gripped his body with both hands as though he felt famine in it already.

"Dead," said Newcomen. "He's gone, Churchill. He's dead on the Hercules Terrace in the garden. Ring the police. Somebody you know. You're sure to know somebody in the police. And then go down to the terrace and make sure that no one disturbs the body until the police come."

He turned his back. Churchill saw the deep wrinkle of strength between the shoulders of his coat as he went out the door.

Hugh Churchill went to the mirror and retied his necktie. He felt a certain shock, but that was because he might find himself out of a job, not because his master was dead.

Then he was telephoning. The Marchese Lucardo was the man. Why he should have chosen police work, why he should have selected a place like little Fiesole, only the marquis himself could tell; and he secured this secret behind the smiling rolls of fat that covered his face.

Before that telephone conversation ended, the Villa Oliviera was alive with footfalls whispering along corridors and thudding downstairs; and Churchill got hastily out of the house.

When he reached the Hercules Terrace he saw Beppo standing hand in hand with Angelina. The daughter, Giulia, and the grandson, Francesco, were beside them. The bearing of burdens made all four stand straight, for a crooked back cannot carry a great weight.

Churchill hurried to them. They gave him one good-morning look and then returned to their contemplation of Thomas Decker. He lay at the side of the water-lily canal, half on his face with his head on his left arm and his knees pulled up a bit, and his right arm lying loosely over the rim of the pool. The clothes were sodden with rain, and the hair roughed by wind and heavy with wet.

Churchill paused three steps away. He did not need to come any closer. Between the shoulders, rather low down, he could see a narrow slit in the dinner jacket of Thomas Decker, and he knew that his employer had been stabbed to death.

Then it seemed to Churchill that he ought to say something. He turned to old Beppo and said: "God save us, Beppo!"

Beppo nodded.

"It will be paid for," he said, and kept looking at Churchill.

Old Angelina crossed herself, as she always did when she had a feeling that her man had said a true thing.

Churchill, suddenly moved by impulse, stepped closer, leaned, and lifted the arm of Decker from the rim of the pool. Even through the wet cloth he felt the warmth of the body. Decker was newly dead.

IT WAS from his study that Thomas Decker had telephoned to Newcomen in Venice, and it was to the study that Newcomen went as soon as he had given instructions to Hugh Churchill. The room was not an essential part of the old villa, but an after-thought added by Decker at the rear of the house for the sake of the north light by which he preferred to view his paintings. To secure his privacy, there was no communication with the main body of the building. The one door, closed with a heavy spring lock, opened on a little path that circled the corner of the house and led to a side entrance.

The key was in the lock. Newcomen turned it. The door gave on a sort of entrance hall where Decker stored bulky objects or new acquisitions which he had not yet appointed to a place. This anteroom opened in turn into the studio proper, where the vaulting sprang nearly forty feet above the concrete floor and all the walls were blank except for the enormous light let into the northern side.

It was a forest of confusion, a junkshop of odds and ends. Racked away against the wall, big canvases turned their ugly backs to the room, a recent purchase of chairs was heaped in a corner, antique tables turned upside down on top of one another, carved consoles and couches, garden sculpture lichened by centuries of exposure, stone vases, medieval capitals curiously worked with masks and animal heads, ancient garden pottery, furnishings from Etruscan tombs, stacks of old upholstery, and a thousand oddities lumbered the floor. A set piece of old battle weapons, from a rusty battle-axe to small poniards, hung on one wall. The air spaces were used also by this collector who had abandoned nothing his fancy hit upon. Some things he had bought because he loved them at any price, and others he accumulated simply because they were cheap. A thousand articles, therefore, dangled from the iron tie-rods which strengthened the upper vaulting. Chandeliers, old lanterns or lantern frames, and whatever was light and bulky, hung in the upper air. The least stir of air or tremor of the building would raise ghostly creakings or faint groanings from the hanging stuff above as it rubbed slightly together.

Toward the centre of the huge room a monstrous easel, adjustable to accommodate canvases of any size, took the north light by day and was furnished with a whole battery of electric globes for night. In front of the easel, half a dozen comfortable chairs were grouped around the place of the owner, where Thomas Decker habitually sat with the telephone on the table beside him. A light battle-axe, missing from the set piece on the wall, lay near the telephone table.

It was not strange, thought Newcomen, that fear should have rubbed elbows with Decker as he sat alone at midnight in this grim warehouse.

He went to the telephone. The wire from it was not buried in the floor but bracketed on top of it under a lead housing—Decker was not always careful about such details—until it disappeared in the wall, on either side of the room. For this was the main telephone wire which served several other instruments in the older portion of the villa. At the outer wall the line had been cut. A single axe-stroke had not cut through the lead and the wire, but several blows had been delivered before the line was severed. That was the reason he had not been able to get the house on the telephone after Decker's call was interrupted.

He went back to the chair of Decker and sat down into it. From an open box on the table, he picked up an English cigarette of hard-rolled Virginia tobacco and lighted it. The taste was sharp in the throat but clean and fresh. Now he saw by chance a green tassel on the floor near his foot. He picked it up absently, and began to draw the sleek of it through his fingers. With his eyes half closed, he reclined in the chair, stripping the silk tassel delicately through his fingers until the police entered the room. Then he stood up as Churchill presented Marchese Lucardo.

THE MARQUIS somewhat resembled the American. Both of them were big, the marquis rather full and loose in flesh and Newcomen smoothed out with solid muscle instead of fat. Each had a broad, good-natured face with an intellectual forehead and a quick eye.

"The commissary of police has asked me to come and make the examination," said Lucardo, "because I have been a friend of poor Thomas Decker for many years. I am only an amateur in these matters, Mr. Newcomen. Forgive me for that; but I try to make up in interest what I lack in professional skill. Have you heard it said that all fat men are amateurs except at the table? However, I shall do my best."

He made an apologetic gesture with his heavy hands, but Newcomen was not deceived. He had regarded not the fat, good-natured smile, but something keenly alert in the eyes of Lucardo. It seemed to him that the shadow of the big man on the floor already was pointing toward the murderer.

Newcomen gave a succinct narrative of everything that had occurred. Lucardo, bowing from time to time, kept examining the room as he listened. His glance rested at last on the axe which lay on the floor near the severed telephone wire. When the narration ended, he said: "You are a lawyer, Mr. Newcomen? No? Such a beautiful piece of clear evidence! Suppose we go back to the words which Mr. Decker spoke over the telephone. He said that yesterday he had seen someone who had frightened him. Can you tell me whether or not he left the house, Mr. Churchill?"

Churchill said that Decker had not stirred from the place.

"Do you know who came to see him?" asked Marchese Lucardo.

"He dined with Nicholas Decker, his cousin, and Aldo Bertelli," said Churchill. "He talked with Dinah Moore while she was working on the frescoes in the chapel, as usual. Miss Nancy Ormonde came in for a cup of tea. He had seen no one else, except yourself, *marchese,* when you called early in the evening. Otherwise, he saw only the servants."

Lucardo knew how to put a world of respect into his voice.

"Shall we suspect the servants?" he asked of the secretary.

"The whole household staff is new. It was cleaned out last month," said Churchill.

"And old servants are the dangerous ones?" smiled Lucardo.

"I think so," said Churchill.

"The gardeners?" asked Lucardo.

"They're faithful—and stupid," said Churchill.

"Fond of Mr. Decker?"

"No one was fond of him," said Churchill. Then he looked at Newcomen and bit his lip.

"Ah, ah, but you don't mean that! Only that he was a little severe with the servants?" murmured Lucardo.

Newcomen glanced at Lucardo sharply.

"I've told you what I know, and I'll leave you now if I may," said he.

"Certainly," agreed the gentle voice. "Only one last thing: When Mr. Decker cried out over the telephone, just before the line went dead, it was as though he had been frightened?"

"Or struck," agreed Newcomen, and went out into the garden, with the green silk tassel still unconsciously gripped inside his left hand.

Lucardo looked at the cigarettes in the open box on the table, but preferred a Turkish brand which he took out of a thin platinum case after giving one to Churchill.

"Won't you sit down, Mr. Churchill?" he said. "Perhaps you'll help me put one and one together. So early in the morning my brain doesn't function very smoothly."

THE TWO agents who accompanied the *marchese* at this point looked at one another steadily, with immobile faces.

"You'll come at the truth soon enough," Churchill said expectantly as he sat down.

"I don't see how," answered Lucardo.

"Between Mr. Decker and Mr. Newcomen," said Churchill, lowering his voice, "you would imagine that everything was perfectly well. But that's not true. Not at all true."

"Ah, and isn't it?" murmured the *marchese,* drawing confidentially nearer. "But really Decker was the guardian of young Mr. Newcomen for a dozen years or so, wasn't he?"

"There was no legal position whatever until recently," snapped Churchill.

"None? Really?"

"Not a bit!" declared Churchill. He moistened his lips, he hurried on. "For those dozen years, until he reached the age of twenty-five, the Newcomen millions were held in trust. He could not touch his money, except for a bit of income paid to him by his bank. During those twelve years, Mr. Decker kept the boy a great deal in this house. He treated him as I never saw Mr. Decker treat any other human being. Gave him the run of the house. Let him order the servants around. Made him his *heir!*"

"Decker had grown fond of the boy; that would explain everything, wouldn't it?" asked the *marchese.*

"Mr. Decker never was fond of anyone!" exclaimed Churchill.

"But what purpose could Mr. Decker have had?" asked Lucardo.

"Purpose? The handling of twelve or fifteen millions is a purpose, isn't it?" cried out Churchill. "And as soon as Mr. Newcomen came of age, he turned over the management of every penny he owns to Mr. Decker."

"Ah? Ah?" murmured the *marchese*. He interrupted himself to say in Italian to his two men: "For fingerprints, please… the axe handle, the telephone." Then he went on: "Interesting. Very, very interesting! As an act of natural gratitude, Newcomen gives the management of his entire estate to his benefactor, his second father, Decker. And then—you're not going to tell me that something went wrong in Decker's investment of the money?"

"I exactly am telling you that!" declared Churchill. "The bank from which the Newcomen millions were snatched away found means of tracing the new investments which Mr. Decker made with the money. Some of those investments seemed strange. The bank sent some odd stories to Mr. Newcomen. He wrote to Mr. Decker about it. Mr. Decker sent back unsatisfactory explanations. And that, in a word, is why Mr. Newcomen made this trip to Italy!"

The secretary sat back in his chair and watched the face of the *marchese* with hungry eyes, and with thirsty hollows puckering in his cheeks. Lucardo wondered over these tidings like a small boy over algebra.

"Imagine the position of Newcomen," said Churchill. "He has placed everything in the hands of a man he cannot trust. He cannot take the management away from Mr. Decker, for a ten-year contract gives Mr. Decker complete control. It is a Gordian knot, you may say. But the knot may be cut. And Mr. Newcomen is a young man capable of action."

"Mr. Churchill!" breathed Lucardo. "Murder? Do you mean that Mr. Newcomen is capable of—"

"Capable of anything!" said Churchill.

He stabbed the air with a vindictive forefinger.

"That wall down there between the lower terrace and the road—when he was hardly fourteen I saw him race a horse over the Diana Terrace and jump it over the wall into the road beneath. Suppose a car had been passing; suppose the horse had smashed a foreleg?

I say, consider what a man like that might do if he found not a matter of jumping a wall but a question of millions? Suppose he *did* telephone to Mr Decker, but it was to ask him to meet him at dawn on the Hercules Terrace?"

"But what a strange request!" said the *marchese*.

"Mr. Newcomen was accustomed to doing strange things in this house. Afterward, he

Marchese Lucardo.

enters the studio, the key was in the door, and hacks the telephone wire in two, doing what he can to place the murder at midnight..."

NEWCOMEN LEFT the villa clear for the police examination. He had breakfast down at the gardener's cottage and afterward sat under the pergola beneath the broad shadows of the grape leaves. Old Beppo put his hands on the shoulders of Newcomen to measure them.

"Now so big! Now so— so—!" said Beppo.

"Take your dirty hands from the *signorino!*" cried Angelina. "Don't you know that he is our *signore*, now?"

She pushed Beppo away and wiped the imaginary stains from the coat of Newcomen with her apron. Newcomen winked at the old gardener, and Beppo laughed with such noisy delight that the old white dog came limping from the shadow and looked up in his master's face.

"Come here, Bianco!" commanded Newcomen. The dog came and stared at him with yellow eyes and slowly wagging tail. "You see? Even Bianco remembers me!"

"Even Bianco?" cried Angelina. "Why, even the chickens know the *signorino* has come home and are ready to run for their lives!"

They laughed together, all three. Bianco whined because he thought they were making fun of him.

"He is still sore in that shoulder. He still limps," said Newcomen.

"What can one do?" demanded Beppo. "God will have his way, and seven days a week, too."

"If a dog loses a toe, that will make it limp also," said Newcomen.

"Oh, no," said Beppo.

"But it's true," insisted Newcomen.

"Listen to him!" said Beppo to his wife. "He says that!"

"If he says it, it is true," declared Angelina. She looked fondly at Newcomen. "Ah, *caro,* the days can be long at the villa without you!"

"But a dog without a toe will not limp," insisted Beppo.

"Have you ever noticed one?" asked Newcomen.

"Just across the way, in the *villino.* A dog—or a wolf. Yes, right there in the *villino.* The American *signorina.* She has one that never leaves her side a moment, day or night. And it does not limp," said Beppo.

"It never leaves her, you say? Who is this *signorina?*" asked Newcomen.

With two fingers Beppo made horns and jabbed them toward the ground and the regions beneath it.

"No, no, Beppo! You must not do that so that people can see," said Angelina.

"Has she the evil eye, really?" asked Newcomen.

"There is no doubt," said Beppo. He made again the horns which keep the devil away so successfully. "Poor young Elia, the son of Martinelli the stone mason... He was robbing birds' nests near the *villino* and the *signorina* scolded him and gave him a glass of milk afterward. And only a week later he fell from a wall and broke his leg!"

"And you knew by that?" asked Newcomen.

"Everyone knew at once, *signorino*. She has some kindly ways, but who can keep the devil from his own?"

Angelina crossed herself and nodded.

"How does she happen to be in the *villino?*" asked Newcomen.

"Ah, she's the one who is retouching the frescoes in the chapel."

"Is she a good artist?"

"What would you have?" asked Angelina. "The devil would not forsake his own, of course. And yet the creature has kind ways about her, too."

Newcomen left by the main gate and went down the road to the *villino* entrance. The driveway made a small circle in front of four columns and three arches, with the upper stories of the house built out over this loggia. He pressed the doorbell and heard the voice-like murmur of it far inside the house. He repeated the ring twice without getting an answer. Then something made him turn sharply about.

A big black German sheep dog stood in the centre of the driveway watching him.

"Come here, boy," said Newcomen, slapping his leg.

The dog watched his hand and did not move. When he stepped forward, it glided back into the brush and stood there, barring an almost invisible path. Newcomen went to the path. The dog backed up step by step. It began to growl softly.

Beyond the shrubbery, a rich Italian voice said: *"La signorina non è casa. Puo ritornare al tocco, per piacere."*

Newcomen took one great stride right at the bared teeth of the dog. It waited until the last instant on crouching legs, before springing back. Newcomen stepped through the hedge of shrubbery onto the lawn that ran down the side of the *villino*.

A girl in a bathing suit lay in a canvas chair, her eyes closed, her face turned to that Italian sun which sears and eats deep, like an acid. Her whole body was as brown as the canvas. He could find no fault with her. She was like something out of the mind.

"*Che cosa ruole?*" she asked sharply, without opening her eyes. He made no answer. The big dog stood before the girl with its head up, its long teeth brightening its grin. A toe was missing from its right forefoot.

IN SPITE of the closeness with which Newcomen watched her, it took him by surprise when he found that her eyes were open. Perhaps that was partly because her hair was so black and her eyes so blue that they seemed more like the trick of a Venetian colorist than a fact in nature.

"Oh Mr. Newcomen," she said, and reached for the dressing gown on the side of the chair.

"Don't get up," said Newcomen. "You're Dinah Moore, aren't you? Have we met anywhere?"

"You never were that far west," said Dinah Moore, relaxing again in the chair and letting the dressing gown slide out of her hand. "But I know you from Tom's descriptions. Tom didn't exaggerate, either, I see," she added, scanning him.

"Do you know what's happened?" said Newcomen.

"Even the birds would chatter Italian rather than let news like that go to waste. That's why I'm taking a last wallop at the sun before I go back to tea parties and post-impressionist and surre-alist fools in New York."

"Tom Decker—it doesn't break you up a great deal, I see."

"Not a great deal," she said.

"Why go back to New York, if you don't like that jungle?"

"I have the price of a steerage ticket now. I won't have it next month."

"Didn't Tom pay you for the work?"

"Tom was one of nature's noblemen—to me. A hundred a week, and found. This is the 'found.'" She hooked a thumb over her shoulder in the direction of the *villino*. She wiggled the thumb to indicate the largeness of the setting. "But I haven't saved much of my pay," she said.

"Why not stay on and keep working at the frescoes?" he asked.

She pulled the green silk of the dressing gown around her. One of the tassels was missing from the belt of it.

Newcomen lighted a cigarette and sat down in the next chair.

"You've never seen my work," she said, draping the gown over her legs.

"I want you to stay."

"There's old New York waiting, and all that career I have to catch up with," said Dinah Moore.

"You'd better stay on here," he insisted.

"For how long?"

"For a week. I want all your time for a week."

"*All* my time?"

"Yes. All the time that you're awake."

She looked at him steadily, making up her mind.

"I'm going back to the steam heat and the jungle," she said.

"I don't think you can afford to give up the job," he told her.

"How much would all my waking hours be worth to you for a week?" she asked.

"More than a hundred dollars," he answered. "Five hundred, say."

"What would I have to do?"

"You'd have to be with me most of the day and part of the night," he said.

"A little compromising, don't you think?"

"In the eyes of Florence? Yes. The foreign colony here would talk its head off, of course."

"Reputation, reputation," she quoted. "You mustn't steal my reputation."

"I don't want to steal it. I want to buy it," he said. "Say for a thousand dollars. One week."

SHE STOOD UP. Newcomen did not rise. He kept looking at the end of the belt from which the green tassel was missing.

"No," she said, shaking her head.

"Sit down," said Newcomen. "I've raised the price to two thousand."

"Good-bye, Anthony."

"Or three thousand, say, for luck."

She turned and walked toward the house briskly.

"Or even four thousand," said Newcomen.

She paused at the corner of the wall. The wolf-dog at her heels whipped around and confronted Newcomen.

"Four thousand in hard cash," said he. "Half of it in advance."

She put out a hand against the wall and her head bowed a little.

"What I mentioned was the *waking* hours," he said.

She turned about, suddenly, as the dog had done.

"What do you want?" she asked.

"Your time, Dinah," said he. "I want your companionship and your conversation."

"What do you want?" she repeated.

"You're not afraid, are you?" he asked.

"Yes, I'm afraid," she said.

"Not of Tony Newcomen."

"Tom Decker was a fool at times, but he was right about you."

"Was Tom really nasty about me? I'm so sorry to hear that."

"You have to come out in the open."

"How can I be more open than this? I'm letting four thousand dollars get away in a week, and I'm not Hollywood."

"Then I'm through!" she stated.

"You're not. As long as you're selling, what do you care about the buying agent?"

She turned about and hurried toward the house.

"Are you really throwing away five thousand dollars?" asked Newcomen.

She stopped again.

"Do come back," he said.

"You said five thousand?" she asked, as she turned.

"Even when you're pale you're lovely, aren't you?" said Newcomen.

She returned slowly.

"But I'm not to deal in personalities, am I?" he asked.

She said nothing.

"Except when we run into silences during the week?" he went on.

"What shall I have to do?" she asked.

"Why, Dinah, I can count your heartbeat in your throat," he answered. "Don't be afraid. There's the same old sun in the same Italian sky. Everything is just as it was five minutes before except that you're five thousand nearer to your heart's desire. You'll have very little to do except be with me. For lunch and dinner. Even for breakfast most of the time. I'm afraid."

"Is that all you'll tell me?" she asked.

"Well, suppose that there were even real danger, eventually," said Newcomen. "It's still far away, far away. It might be at the very end of the seventh day. And of course it might not be at all."

She swallowed, making such an effort that her hand rose part way to her throat.

"And for a brave, free spirit like yours, accustomed to taking chances, seven days will not be an eternity, eh?" said Newcomen. "Do sit down—no, not way over there. Take this chair beside me."

She took the chair beside him.

WHEN NEWCOMEN got back to the house he found Nicholas Decker in the library with his soft, manicured hands and his wig and his high color that always looked the brightness and the texture of rouge.

He waved casually to Newcomen and then shook his hand.

"Well, it happened, Tony," he said. "I always warned him. I always told him that it would happen, sooner or later. Too many enemies. A man can't go on breeding poison all the days of his life. Sooner or later he goes down, Have you seen the will?"

"Tom Decker's will?" asked Newcomen. "No. What about it?"

"Lucardo dug it out, right away. It's worth seeing. A lot of legacies. Aldo Bertelli and Lucardo and even poor Nicholas Decker are all mentioned for good bits. Twenty thousand to me. Transfigure that into lire and it's quite a sum. The main split is to Nancy Ormonde, though. Confounded lucky girl! She gets the *villino* with all the buildings around it and the land attached to it, to say nothing of a hundred thousand in hard cash. Think of that! Everything that's left, including the Oliviera, goes to you, of course. We expected that. But what a wedge Nancy's share cuts out of your pie!"

"The *villino* and a hundred thousand dollars?" asked Newcomen, thoughtfully.

"Exactly. A hundred thousand. That's motive enough for a murderer, isn't it?"

"Did *you* do it, Nicholas?" asked Newcomen.

"I? Did I kill him? I often used to wonder why I didn't put an end to him," said Decker. "Wallowing in wealth and never a penny to pay the silly little debts that made me wretched. But I put off the day and now someone has done it for me. Who do you think, Tony?"

"Dinah Moore," said Newcomen, "or Nancy Ormonde, or Bertelli, or Marchese Lucardo, or you. Someone that he saw yesterday, it seems. Five suspected people. Or else I could have done it when I came this morning. I entered the place in an unusual way, over the terraces. Perhaps I met him on the Hercules Terrace and stabbed him in the back."

"Did you?" said Decker, nodding in the most sympathetic way. "Is it true that Tom mismanaged the Newcomen millions to such a degree that you were desperate?"

"Churchill would be saying that, I suppose," smiled Newcomen. "Dear old Hugh! What a comforter he is about a house! I suppose that Lucardo will get to the bottom of the mystery before long."

"Lucardo? Get to the bottom of it? My dear lad, poor Franco is the most inefficient man in Italy. Sad case, too. Good family. Sweet manners; really sweet. Sympathetic. Charming. Enough money to keep his house open part of the year. But his brain rotted away by idleness and detective stories."

"He's gone, is he?" asked Newcomen.

"An empty shell. That's all," said Nicholas Decker. "Just a sort of fat Sherlock, twiddling his thumbs, asking questions, probing into the dark corners. The police like to use him, however, and with their help he does occasionally turn up something. When anything is uncovered, he gets some credit. He is of a famous old family and the police permit him to hang around."

"Not a fellow to have done a murder, is he? He wouldn't have a motive, I suppose?" asked Newcomen.

HE SAT DOWN on the big table, so worm-eaten and time-softened that it seemed ready to give way under the burden of him. His hand found the sleek of a little cat-headed Egyptian goddess, carved in diorite, and began to caress it.

"Murder? He's had his duels and all that. Murder? Oh, I don't know. And there's money for a motive. Owed Tom a devilish lot of money, for one thing. In the second place, Tom's will gives him ten or twelve thousand. Oh, no, I wouldn't rule Lucardo out from among the suspects. Don't do that, Tony! You mustn't be hasty!"

"Leave him in, then. Among the people Tom saw yesterday there are Dinah Moore, and Nancy Ormonde, and Bertelli. That completes the list. What about Bertelli?"

"You know him, don't you?"

"I've always been too young to know him well."

"That's true," said Nicholas Decker. "He's one of the old souls, of course. I'll tell you what you do. Just see if you find among Tom's papers any notes signed by Bertelli, will you? Might be interesting. Both owed him money. Tons of it. More than he'd ever let *me* owe him, for instance."

"I'll look into it," said Newcomen. "What about Nancy Ormonde?"

"Well, what about her? You know about Nancy, of course. Tom brought her over here to Italy. That was a whole year ago. He's kept her waiting ever since. To come expecting to marry millions, and then find that she's wasted her time and that her chances are gone. That might drive a girl to almost anything. Lately she's been consoling herself with Bertelli. And now the legacy will give her a chance to breathe freely for a while."

"How did her chances go?" asked Newcomen.

"Why, this Dinah Moore came along and put her evil eye on Tom and he couldn't resist her. I'll tell you about Dinah. She—"

"Don't bother," said Newcomen. "I've seen her."

"Have you? A look was enough, eh? To talk of something else for half a moment, Tony, old boy—now that you're the head of the family—I mean, in Tom's place, d'you see—the fact is that I'm horribly broke until my legacy is paid. If I don't have a thousand dollars by tomorrow I'll be in such hell—"

"I have a thousand lire," said Newcomen.

"I said dollars, Tony," answered Decker.

"I know you did," said Newcomen. "But here are the lire, if you can use them."

"That's decent of you," said Decker, pocketing the money. "It gives me a day to turn around, at least. A chance to keep on fighting for a round or two."

An automatic banged four times in rapid succession; a man screamed; voices rattled and feet ran inside and outside the house.

"That's Lucardo at work!" cried Decker.

They went outside and found Lucardo's two agents holding a

man who was shouting in loud Italian. "He lies! He always lies! He never does anything but lie! I wasn't here last night. My fiancée—I was with her!"

Lucardo sat down on the edge of a huge pot that contained the twisted trunk and crooked branches of a lemon tree.

"I've just telephoned to your *fidanzata,* Emilio," he said. "She tells me that you left her at ten-thirty."

"She? She says that?" screamed Emilio. "It is because she wants that Taddeo Spinucci, that farmer in—"

"Emilio, be still," said Lucardo.

EMILIO WAS still. The agents dragged him close to the *marchese's* fuming cigarette.

"Here is Lorenzo," said Lucardo, pointing to the tall, cadaverous butler. "He says that he was here with you at this house, last night, between eleven and twelve. The rain came down with a crash and you both stepped into the hall of the studio because the door was unlocked. You were only waiting for the rain to stop falling so heavily. After a while you began to talk about the way *Signor* Decker discharged you a month ago. You told Lorenzo that you hated *Signor* Decker and that he cheated you when he paid your wages. And then you pushed open the heavy door that leads into the studio and you looked in and saw *Signor* Decker. Afterward, two or three minutes later, while you still stood in a corner waiting for the rain to end, *Signor* Decker suddenly came out of his study and walked past you into the garden. A moment later, you said good-bye to Lorenzo and left the house, although the rain was falling heavily. Is that true?"

"*Signor* Marchese, may God never be kind to me if I tell anything but the truth," protested Emilio. "This Lorenzo, I knew his older brother and his father before him. In Siena they are famous for their lies and—"

"Did you find a knife?" asked Lucardo of his two men.

One of them held up a slender leather case and drew from it a sort of miniature poniard with a four-inch blade that came to such a fine point that the light seemed to distill and fall from it in drops.

Emilio sank through the hands of the agents to his knees.

"*Signor* Marchese," he said in a pitiful voice, "believe me—be a father to poor Emilio... I have been an honest man, except with cards. I never have done a wrong thing except a little bit with dice. I am not a liar."

"I want to believe you, poor Emilio," said Lucardo in the softest of voices. "Tell me, therefore..."

"It is true that the black devil was in me," said Emilio. "And when I went out into the garden in the rain, I hoped to kill him. The wine that I put in my mouth that night had taken all my brains down my throat. My good saint had forgotten me. I ran through the dark of the night with the knife in my hand. Then I saw him. He went slowly. I stole up behind him. I followed him down to the Hercules Terrace. He came to the edge of the water lilies. It was very dark. And how the rain came in my face! It cooled me. I could think. I saw the thing I was about to do. And then I went away. The farther I went, the faster I ran. I swore that I never would take the knife in my hand again! And I left *Signor* Decker standing there in the dark by the side of the pool and I did not touch him. The saints can see me. They can see my soul like the palms of these hands. They know I am telling the truth."

"You swore never to take the knife in your hand again, and yet it was with you today," pointed out the *marchese.*

"True, *Signor* Marchese, but who can give up an old friend all in a moment?" asked Emilio.

He had worked so hard with his speech that beads of sweat stood out everywhere on his wedge-shaped, sallow face. More words kept swelling in his throat, though second thought kept them unuttered. The sweat ran down over his lips and he blew it away with each laboring breath.

"When *Signor* Decker came out of the study, what was in his face?" asked the *marchese.*

"He looked," said Emilio, "like a man who is going to collect rents."

"You, Lorenzo," said the *commissariato.* "What did *Signor* Decker seem to you?"

"He seemed to me a man who had felt a great fear and he was hurrying away from it," said Lorenzo.

"Did you see his eyes?" asked the *marchese.*

"I saw his eyes," said Lorenzo, "and they looked back at me and did not see me. They were empty."

"They were empty because he was thinking of something else and therefore could not see anything except his thought," said Emilio.

"He was very tired," said Lorenzo. "He had the look one sees in a man who has been up all night long. He was hunched over, a little. He looked two inches shorter than usual."

"That was because he was hurrying," said Emilio. "When a man hurries, his long steps sink him closer to the ground."

"He was afraid," insisted Lorenzo. "He dared not look behind him, for fear of what he might see. When he came to the door, he leaned against it for a moment."

"Tell me about that," broke in Lucardo. "He leaned there against the door," said Emilio, "while he made himself ready to go out into the rain. Everyone stops a moment before going into the rain."

"Very well," said Lucardo. "Take Emilio away. I think he will pay for this murder in the end."

"No! *Signor* Marchese… Mercy! Do not accuse me! The men you accuse always die!"

They dragged Emilio away. His screams remained the rest of the day in the ears of all who heard them.

"SO IT ENDS?" said Newcomen to the *marchese.* "And you've found the guilty fellow at a stroke!"

Lucardo shrugged his shoulders slowly, and lifted his hands with the palms turned up. He seemed to expect an answer from the sun-drenched sky.

"But you, *Signor* Newcomen?" he asked, with that soft-voiced courtesy of his.

"I think of one or two things," said Newcomen. "When Tom Decker came to the Hercules Terrace, why did he pause there in the darkness beside the water lilies?"

"True. It is very odd. No one stands still in the rain," said Lucardo. "But you think that Emilio told a part of the truth? You think, actually, that he told a part of it?"

"Undoubtedly," said Newcomen. "Lies always are rather clever. Even a child lies well. But the picture of a mature, intelligent man like Thomas Decker standing there by the lily pads in the darkness that would be a stupid, pointless lie. No Italian would say that unless it were true."

"You touch on the main point. Why did he linger there by the water lilies until he was stabbed through the back?"

"Well, what's your theory?" asked Newcomen.

"Theory? Ah, I never have a theory," said Lucardo. "I go about this work like a child picking up pebbles. I find what I can, get it all together, and then hope that it will arrange itself into some sort of a pattern. You see I'm hopelessly an amateur."

No one watched the pair of big men more closely than Hugh Churchill. Afterward he found a chance to say to Newcomen: "You don't trust Marchese Lucardo, I see."

"I hope he didn't think that," said Newcomen.

Hugh Churchill frowned and waved a finger of warning at the whole Italian world.

He said: "You're quite right. I've observed the *marchese* for a long time. Some people think he's a foolish fellow. But I consider him a dangerous man; very dangerous."

"Look through Decker's accounts, will you?" asked Newcomen,

after he had considered this warning for a moment. "See if there are any promissory notes signed by Lucardo, or by Bertelli, or by Nicholas Decker, will you?"

The hungry face of Churchill sharpened to a point.

"Instantly!" he cried, and went off at once with his long-stepping, scrawny legs.

OVER THE repaired telephone line Newcomen said to Dinah Moore: "You'll come up to lunch, won't you? "

"Yes," she answered.

"One o'clock? No, make it twelve-thirty and we'll have a look at the chapel, first of all."

"If you wish," she said.

"By the way, I think it would save time all around if you packed some bags and moved into the villa for a few days. I can give you a suite to yourself and your maid. Then I could have you at hand day or night."

She was silent.

"You might make the move this morning, in fact," he added, crisply.

"The bargain is that I have to take orders from you about every tiling for seven days. Are you ordering me to the villa now?"

"You don't want to come?"

"Please don't make me!"

"Would you be grateful if I let you off?"

"Terribly, terribly grateful."

He waited a moment.

"I'll expect only you," he ended, "and not your bags."

"Thank you," she said.

He waited again, and then rang off on the silence. Displeasure in his face rarely appeared as a scowl; and now he seemed merely a bit thoughtful as he pushed the bell and asked for his car.

He was slipping in under the wheel when Churchill ran out

to him, breathing deeply with haste and excitement. He gripped the edge of the automobile with his two skinny hands and talked close to the ear of Newcomen.

"To my personal knowledge, there were notes signed by all three, particularly by Lucardo and Bertelli. Notes for thousands of dollars. Thousands and thousands! And every one of them has been taken out of the safe. Every one is gone!"

CHURCHILL PULLED back his head so as to view Newcomen's face and judge the effect of the news.

"Who had the combination of the safe?" asked Newcomen.

"Only Mr. Decker."

"And you?"

"Why—naturally—of course... I..."

"I'll talk it over later," said Newcomen, and drove on.

He slid the car down the long slope. The sun had burned away the last of the morning mist and left the face of Florence naked, with Brunelleschi's dome like a noble forehead above the lesser features. He passed through the narrow old streets where pedestrians have eyes for everything except automobiles and ears for everything except automobile horns. Through the Porta Romana he took the long ascent that carried him beyond the village of Arcetri to a little villa that kept the top of a hill for itself.

It had a warm, pink face. The flowers of the climbing jasmine thickened the air with sweetness. After the glare of the outdoors, the interior of the house offered the damp coolness of a cave. It was not a large building, but it gave some arched vistas, and so many flowers bloomed in pots and vases that the fragrance of a garden breathed in every room, and some of the humid smell of wet garden soil also.

Nancy Ormonde came into the salon. She had red hair and green eyes, therefore she was wearing a dress of green chiffon as cool as a mountain breeze. She hurried to Newcomen and shook his hand.

"I saw you come up in the car," she said. "Sit down here, Tony. This gives you a better view of the garden and the mountains, or does the garden seem too hot to look at? I don't know what I'm doing in Florence so late in the year. But Tom Decker—I don't want to talk about that; you don't mind if I don't talk about that, do you?"

"You were going to marry Tom, weren't you?" he asked.

"I was thinking about it. Girls who have to make their living are apt to think about almost anything," she remarked. "Did you know that?"

"When a man gets to be twenty-five, he has to know things like that," said Newcomen.

"But after I'd been in Italy for a while, where the day is fifty hours long instead of Hollywood's ten, I began to think that after all there might be time and leisure enough to find the right man, not just the man's money."

"Did you break off with him?" asked Newcomen.

"It wasn't a break," she said, thoughtfully. "It was more of a pull. A pull apart."

She illustrated with her hands. Newcomen watched with pleasure, for the hands were small and lovely.

"What I'm wondering," he said, "is if you'll come back with me and have lunch."

"I'd love to, but I can't. I've already promised."

"It's Bertelli, isn't it?" he asked. "He has the sort of a face that intelligent women are apt to love. Go and make excuses to Bertelli, Nancy, will you?"

She looked for a moment through the window, over the garden, at the grey-blue of the mountains.

"Well," she said. "I suppose I must do as you say."

SHE LEFT the room. Newcomen did not look at the view through the window, but at the blankness of the wall, studying it as though he found a picture of a most intricate pattern outlined upon it.

When Nancy Ormonde came down again, she was wearing a black dress even more filmy than the green. She had on a wide-brimmed hat.

"You're still where I left you," she said. "What have you been thinking about?"

He looked at her.

"Tell Nancy," she said, laughing.

"I was thinking that I like emeralds better for you than diamonds," said Newcomen.

"A diamond is better with black, you know," she said. Then she broke off to add: "Do you notice *every*thing, Tony?"

"You *are* pretty,"

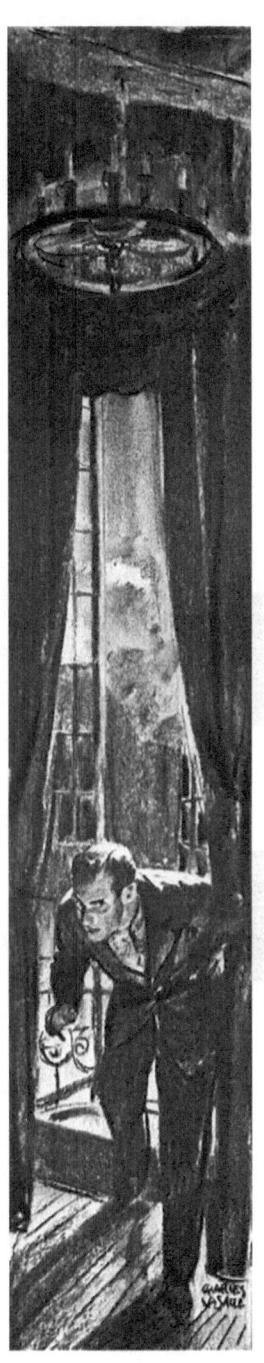

A man glided swiftly into the heavy murk of the room. Motionless, Dinah watched him from the balcony.

said Newcomen. "You're the real thing. When you find the right man, Nancy, don't let him be poor. You ought to have champagne and gardenias and the whole works."

"I wonder," said Nancy.

When they got in the open car, he drove softly because of the wide brim of her hat. She kept holding it with one hand, which made her seem childishly young. To keep out the glare of the sun, she closed her eyes.

"Tell me why you came up here for me so suddenly," she said.

"I'm the spoiled son of a rich man. I always want the best," he answered.

"And of course you're twenty-five, too," she suggested.

"Exactly twenty-five years old," said Newcomen.

"I like you," said Nancy, with her eyes still closed. "I like you a lot."

"Now that I've grown up, you mean?"

"Yes, now that you've grown up. As a boy, you were horrible."

She began to laugh to herself, looking straight ahead, remembering things.

The car shot up the hill to San Domenico and Newcomen sent the cypresses of the Decker driveway whizzing behind him.

"The Decker place is all yours, now, isn't it?" said Nancy Ormonde, as she stepped out. "Are we having lunch alone?"

"Well, there's Dinah Moore. Does she count?"

"Count? I'd count her twice, wouldn't you?" asked Nancy Ormonde.

"Tom didn't," said Newcomen. "He left her out of his will."

But they were inside the house now, and that made a convenient gap in the conversation. The lofty hall was sure to stop the mind for a moment, and the stone lion at the foot of the great stairs glowered at them with 400 years of sour constraint. The butler said that the *Signorina* Moore was working in the chapel.

"I'll stay here," said Nancy Ormonde.

"Are you afraid of Dinah?" asked Newcomen.

"Yes, aren't you?" she answered. "But I'll come along anyway."

"I thought the two of you would get on like nothing at all," said Newcomen as they went through the huge chambers of the house, all filled with the hodgepodge commercial air, the museum effect that collectors achieve in spite of themselves. "I thought you'd like one another."

"Did you?" said Nancy. "That doesn't sound quite twenty-five, Tony. Haven't they told you yet that she stole Tom from me?"

"Is that the popular version?" he asked.

"It's not popular with me," she said.

"Do you dislike her, really?"

"I'll tell you what," confided Nancy, "it makes me feel quite helpless when I see men bowled over by a pair of long legs and a good golf swing and a fine forehand drive. I feel as though I'd lost my grasp on the situation."

"Her legs *are* long," said Newcomen. "There's that much truth in what you say."

"Tony, is she meaning a lot to you?"

"Of course she is. If she were only a picture on the wall, she'd mean a lot."

"Well, I wish her nothing but freckles and bad luck," said Nancy.

SHE BEGAN to laugh, and she knew how to laugh so delightfully that no one could help joining her. Then he pushed open a little arched door set flush with the wall and they stepped into the chapel. Dinah Moore, on her knees in a corner, dressed in an old working smock, was working up the color at the bottom of one of the frescoes.

"Think of the Eighteenth Century turning all this into a mere prettiness," said Nancy Ormonde, looking up at the big liernes of the vaulting.

"The Eighteenth Century wanted rooms for conversation, not to pray in," said Newcomen.

"That's rather nice. Did you hear that, Dinah?" asked Nancy Ormonde. She was repeating the remark as she shook hands, but Dinah Moore made no comment. The wolf-dog came out of the shadows and stood beside her.

"This is the Oliviera sin," said Dinah, waving toward the walls, with the frescoes walking all around them.

"It looks like first-rate decoration to me," said Newcomen.

"It is first-rate," said Dinah, "it's worth all the rest of the house and everything in it, unless I restore it to death. But I'm trying to bring up the old color out of the stucco and add nothing. What do you think?"

She pointed toward the central part of a "holy wedding" which she had finished and which shone out from the dim centuries that had tarnished the rest of the walls.

"It looks a good deal more Renaissance than Bible, but that was the fashion in Florence," said Newcomen. "Where's the Oliviera sin that you were talking about?"

"We've just found out," said Dinah Moore. "The sin was that

the Olivieras had themselves painted in the holy roles. Joseph is really the Conte di Fosdinovo; and the bride is a portrait of poor Beatrice Oliviera. Most of the others were real people who were at the wedding."

"I wouldn't pity Beatrice though, would you?" asked Nancy. "She was a real Oliviera."

"The way I remember it," said Newcomen, "they were Spaniards from up Burgos way, or something like that."

"They stuck at nothing," said Nancy Ormonde. "They used bribery, knives, and poison all the way to the titles that they finally wore; but in the windup they all died by the same knives and poison. The whole tribe of them had black hair and blue eyes. Like Dinah."

Newcomen looked at the black hair of Dinah Moore. He could not see the blue of her eyes because she had leaned just then to pat the head of the dog.

"That Beatrice has a charming face though," said Newcomen, going closer to the painting.

"All the Olivieras had charm," said Nancy. "But poor Fosdinovo! Six months after the wedding Beatrice embraced him one day, and while she was holding his arms her lover came up behind and stuck a knife into his back. That was true Oliviera." She added: "Ah, I shouldn't have said that. I'm sorry, but I forgot about poor Tom."

"We have thick skins; it's all right," answered Newcomen. "Shall we go in to lunch?"

They had lunch in the dining room with a pair of wooden thirteenth century saints looking mournfully down on them from the corners and some portrait busts in painted stucco occupying niches in the walls. Dinah Moore was very quiet. She did little more than smile once or twice, but when she lifted her eyes Anthony guessed by the largeness of the pupils that she was afraid. Of what, he could not guess.

"It seems strange, doesn't it?" said Nancy Ormonde. "I mean, just the three of us in this great room. It's as though something were about to happen. Or as though we had met for a purpose. It's like a stage set. What do you think, Dinah?"

It was in fact as though she had spoken a cue on the stage, for just then someone cried out in the pantry; voices rattled like breaking dishes.

"Find out what's happening, Lorenzo," said Newcomen to the butler.

Lorenzo silenced the babble of voices in the pantry. He came back to announce: "Emilio has tried to commit suicide in the prison. His guilt is certain now, *signore*."

Newcomen, as he listened, looked not at the butler but at his two guests. In every gesture and attitude they had been different enough until this point, but now, as they heard the words of Lorenzo, each of them looked down and it seemed to Newcomen that in each he detected an air of definite relief.

DINAH MOORE, very late that afternoon, walked on the Hercules Terrace after the shadows from the western trees covered this level of the garden with a false twilight. Before sunset, she sat on one of the stone benches near the canal of water lilies and considered for a long time the big coarse blossoms as they folded for the night. The canal, running down the centre of the terrace, terminated in one of those extravagant old grottoes which the Italians loved so much, the dark gullet of it dripping with sponge stone like teeth in the mouth of a shark. With a searching eye she studied the whole canal, and stood for a time at the entrance to the grotto. It was big enough to have hidden a dozen men in its artificial cavern. When the sun sank, she went back to the *villino* in time to answer the jangle of the telephone.

It was Newcomen's voice, saying: "This evening we'll go up to Impruneta, if you don't mind, and dine on the terrace. I'd take you up myself except that I have an appointment that puts me out of your way. Take a taxi and be up there in a half hour or so, please."

When she hung up and turned from the telephone, she saw the dog standing at the pantry door with his nose close to the crack of it. She pushed the door open almost in the face of her cook. The sour little man jerked off his tall white cap and his eyes opened with a sudden fear.

"Who pays you, Roberto?" she asked.

"Honored *signorina,* it is you who pays me," he said.

"I pay you for cooking," she answered. "But who pays you for spying on me, Roberto; for listening at my bedroom door and sneaking through the garden behind me?"

"Ah, *signorina,* as true as there is blue in heaven—"

"You are free for the evening. I am dining out," she said.

She let the door swing shut and went up to her bedroom. The warmth of the day still was in it, so she opened the French windows that gave on the balcony and allowed the evening breeze to enter with the thin resinous scent of the pine trees. Afterward, she bathed, dressed, and telephoned to a taxi. Then she turned out the lights.

The bedchamber, which she used also as a living room when she was alone, had served as a studio for other occupants of the *villino* and ran up through the two top stories of the building. By a flight of stairs and a balcony, it communicated with the servants' rooms of the third story. She descended to the front door, locked it, and at the same time heard the voices of Roberto and his wife departing from the rear of the house. After that, she returned to her bedroom and climbed the stairs with her dog to the balcony that jutted out from the inner wall. She always had wanted a sunset view from one of the southern windows of the little upper bedrooms, and there would never be a better time to have a glimpse of it.

She climbed slowly to the balcony of the great room, enjoying the thick twilight dusk that filled the house. The dog went with her, and as they reached the balcony it was his sudden start that made her look down. There had not been a sound, but now she saw the silhouette of a man glide from the outer balcony swiftly into the heavy murk of the room.

She shrank down behind the high arm of a couch which was almost the only furnishing of the upper balcony. Her dog, Hans, following, touched her face with the cold of his wet nose. She whispered, and he crouched beside her.

A FINGER of light began to move in the chamber like a bright fish in the shadowy depths of water. It ran faintly over the polish of the table, brought one winking flash of brilliance from a mirror, and then touched here and there on the ceiling just above her. She realized that the intruder, with a soundless footfall, was climbing the stairs toward her balcony. Hans realized it also. She felt the growl vibrating in his throat before it was audible, and gripped him hard by the muzzle. She made herself small, crushing the dog to her with one arm; then the ray of the flashlight slid down the balcony floor and turned the waxed tiles to shimmering red glass.

The light disappeared. Still she held her breath. Hans was quivering. The searcher might well have seen her dress beneath the couch, and perhaps was coming on now silently in the darkness.

She drew one great breath when the torch flared again in the depths of the room. Quietly, by inches, she approached again the verge of the balcony; the light had settled down at her desk in the farther corner of the room, and as the full eye of the pocket flash remained open, its reflection from the stucco wall set off the outlines of the man in high clear relief. She saw the big head and the unmistakable shoulders of Newcomen.

He started at the lower drawers of the desk, first. She never had been able to move them without drawing groans from the ill-fitted wood, but Newcomen's touch maneuvered them in an oiled silence. Even when his hands dipped into the stacks of papers, not a rustle, not a whisper, came to her straining ears.

The dog beside her began to pant with the heat. She tapped it between the eyes and the faint noise ended.

The lower drawers were finished quickly by that rapid searcher. He ran through the small upper compartments.

Dinah Moore stood up. Even the slightest noise, she was sure, would reach the ears of that huntsman below. She dared not risk the scratching of the dog's nails on the tiles. She picked up the solid hundred pounds of the dog and carried him. There was a long interval of strain before she could open the door of the hall. Distrusting the rusted hinges, she pushed the door open gradually, bit by bit, and then, entering the hall, slowly closed it behind her.

When at last the latch had engaged without a click and she could let Hans slip to the floor, she leaned her hands against the wall and her forehead against her hands, breathing deeply until the tremor was gone from her muscles. After that she moved down the length of the darkening hall, down the turnings of the rear staircase, into the hot steaming odors of the kitchen, and so to the rear door.

At the last instant, it slipped from the tips of her fingers and closed with a jarring impact.

She held her breath, listening, counting seconds; at last she left the *villino* and hurried down the road to stop her taxicab before it entered the driveway.

WHAT NEWCOMEN had settled on at the desk was an unsigned note dated two days before and written in the familiar hand of Thomas Decker. In the long terms of his schooldays, how welcome a sight that swift scrawl had been on the face of an envelope!

The note began without any introductory phrase.

It said:

Well, let's admit at once that he's everything you say. That makes him worth a real investment, I think. I'm willing to pay for him, but you must repay. You definitely must. If this sentiment revolts you—well, then *I* would revolt you. And we might as well have an understanding now. Being a businessman, I feel that I should have something in hand for my effort and for my restraint. An ultimatum is an ugly thing. On the other hand, prolonged suspense is disgusting to a man of my age and mental habits. So let's decide one way or the other, quickly.

If you say no, I'm sorry for your man in America, but I'm much sorrier for myself. I've opened the door of my heart to a great hope. To a spring wind. To the expectation of a glorious new happiness. But I can't keep the door ajar forever. I have to know now whether the happiness is going to enter, or if it is only a tantalizing hope.

My dear, I am pouring out my spirit toward you in these words. Trust me, I shall find your happiness.

The future should open to you, now, as the world opens to a man on a mountain-top. Consider everything. Think of time in the aggregate and don't consider little retail moments. From that point of view, youth becomes a matter of terminology rather than of important fact.

What I trust in is the profound good sense which is in you and which you can use if you will. Distrust the passionate reactions of the moment. There are numerous differences between man and woman. Thank God there is one divine similarity. It is the mind which exists in both.

This note the swift small hand of Thomas Decker had placed on a single page of ordinary letter paper. Newcomen read it once, closed his eyes, glanced through it again, and had it by heart.

He was refolding the paper when he heard from the rear of the house a slight jarring noise, an impact rather than a sound. It got him swiftly to his feet. He remained stooped over the desk for a moment, listening. Then he replaced the note in the exact place from which he had taken it, closed the desk, and let the pocket torch stare down on the surface of it for a moment. The blotter, which was slightly awry, he straightened with his gloved fingers, gave the room a final circular sword-slash with the narrowed ray of the light, and then left as he had come, stepping onto the outer balcony, swinging over the edge of it, and so down one of the pillars of the front loggia to the ground.

A moment or two later he was rushing his long-nosed car down from San Domenico toward the twinkling lake of Florence lights.

He parked his car near the entrance to the Bellavista Restaurant and walked into the dimness of the lower hall.

"Is a lady here waiting for a *Signor* Newcomen?" he asked of the doorman.

"Yes, *signore*," said the doorman.

"How long ago did she arrive?" asked Newcomen.

"Twenty minutes ago, *signore;* or fifteen, at least."

Newcomen gave him twenty lire.

"How long ago did she come?" he asked.

The doorman soothed the wrinkles of the two little bills with his fingertips and studied the face of Newcomen. Then he smiled down at the money.

"Two minutes. No more, *signore.*"

Newcomen went up the stairs.

BREATHING A bit from the long climb, Newcomen came out on the terrace. It was a bit too early. Only a few tables were occupied, and the waiters moved with a look of hungry eagerness, uncertain what the evening would bring them.

Dinah Moore sat in a black dress at a table in the southern angle. She must have hurried up those stairs at full speed and she still was breathing a little deeply.

"You've been here twenty minutes, the boy tells me," said Newcomen. "How you must have hurried! I'm sorry."

She smiled and shrugged her shoulders, as serene as the bright open face of the night. Next she was ordering carefully, considering the meagre choices which were offered without haste, but in spite of her outward calm, Newcomen guessed at fear behind her eyes. Hans, the wolf-dog, was with her. He had risen when she rose, and showed his teeth to Newcomen. He sank down again when his mistress sat; but though he was out of sight, he could not be out of mind.

"Are you afraid of Hans?" she asked. "I mean, laying your professional manhood aside."

"Yes, I'm afraid of the blighter."

"Why?"

"Well, he's not like other dogs. Not quite."

"And you're not like other men. Not quite."

"Very badly different?" he asked.

She laid a hand against the soft of her throat and looked at his big, broad-fingered hands.

"Very different," she decided finally.

"Ruthless. You mean that, don't you?"

She smiled at him. "We're going to be pleasant, aren't we?" she asked.

The waiter brought them cold consommé.

"I want to see the proprietor," said Newcomen.

"He is the cook also, *signore,* and he is very busy," said the waiter.

"He has his wife to take charge for a moment. Tell him to put on a clean apron and a fresh hat and come up here an instant, will you?"

The waiter went off.

"What do you think I'm after, these days?" he asked.

"You're trying to find out who killed Tom Decker...."

"Ah?"

"Or to take the blame away from yourself."

"No one cared a rap about Tom Decker. Why should I go after the murderer?" he asked.

"Perhaps you're on the trail simply because you like the hunt."

"But the trail has ended, Dinah. Lucardo got Emilio at once. The poor guilty devil practically confessed by trying to commit suicide in jail."

"I sympathize with frightened people."

Newcomen stared at her; then the proprietor appeared.

"You wished to see me, *Signor* Newcomen?"

"Ah, yes," said Newcomen. "You know *Signor* Bertelli and *Signor* Nicholas Decker?"

"Certainly, *signore*. That is my great pleasure."

"Last night they were up here until eleven, I understand?"

"Until eleven? Yes, yes, *signore*. They were here."

"And then I understand that they left? A few minutes after eleven?"

"Yes, *signore*."

"You're sure of that, aren't you?" asked Newcomen.

"Oh, perfectly sure."

"Someone else saw them and noticed the time?"

"My wife, *signore*. She happened to look at the clock and mentioned that it was ten past eleven when they left."

"You couldn't possibly be mistaken?"

"By no means, *signore*."

"Beyond any question, it was ten after eleven when the two of them left?"

"Exactly so, *signore*," said the proprietor.

"It was I who suggested, a moment ago, that they had left at eleven. I said I had heard they left at that hour. But entirely independently of me, you remember the time?"

"Oh, certainly, *signore*."

"Now isn't it a fact that they left after twelve? Remember carefully. Wasn't it after twelve?" asked Newcomen.

THE PROPRIETOR started to shake his head and smile when a sudden thought struck and shook him.

"Twelve!" he gasped. "Twelve... I think... Heaven forgive me! Of course it was after twelve."

"Very well. That's all I wanted to know," said Newcomen dryly.

"*Signore,* I wish to say—"

"Never mind," said Newcomen. "I've heard what you have to say. That's all—for this evening. And good night."

The proprietor still hesitated for a moment and then took his way slowly off among the tables, pausing once or twice to put his hand on the back of a chair and then continue, his head weighted down by thought.

"Aldo Bertelli and even Nicholas Decker—they're both to be suspects from now on?" asked the girl.

"Suspects? Why should they be?" asked Newcomen.

"It seems they bought an alibi from the proprietor here," she answered. "A twelve o'clock alibi. Now you've smashed that all to pieces. Their alibi is gone. The open season on Bertelli and Nicholas Decker has started. Isn't that it?"

"The fact simply is," said Newcomen, "that I heard a rumor round the town that Bertelli and Nicholas had alibis, at least. *They* would never be involved in any suspicion. They had been up here at Impruneta that evening until midnight. So I thought I'd enquire. Isn't that harmless? And what could I do with what I've just learned even if that were a fact?" he asked.

"You could telephone to that clever devil, Lucardo, for one thing," she said.

"Yes, of course I could do that. But is Lucardo really as clever as you say or is he a simple fellow, as most people believe?"

"One way or the other," said Dinah Moore, "you've made up your mind about him, and nothing that I can say will change you."

"Do you know something, Dinah?"

"Well?" she asked.

"You're careless. You don't stay behind the veil. But of course you don't understand what I mean by that."

"I think I do," she said.

"Tell me, then. What *do* I mean?"

"That I'm talking too openly; too like a man. Isn't that it?"

"Something like that, perhaps. There is a bit of mystery, you know, that a girl puts on and off when she pleases. At the unexpected moment she slips behind a smile and disappears from the man's ken. But I suppose that you despise tricks like that?"

"No. I've used the trick. Every woman does until she meets an eye that's likely to see through her. Fundamentally, though, it isn't a trick at all, but you wouldn't understand, Anthony."

"Shall I ever understand?"

"No, I don't think so," said the girl.

"This is exciting; tell me why I'll never know."

"Were you ever in love?" she asked.

"Of course. Twenty times."

"There's my answer," said the girl. "Twenty times. That means never."

"Stuff and nonsense," said Newcomen. "I've been dizzy about one girl or another since I was ten years old."

"And did you have little chills up the spine?" she asked. "And when you met her was it like stepping into cold water—so that you lost your breath?"

"Exactly!" said Newcomen. "Oh, I know all about that!"

"I knew you did," said the girl.

"Ah, come, Dinah! You mean that I've missed the big thing?"

"Completely."

"Tell me what it is. If it's beyond me, I'll confess that I've never scratched the surface of life."

She shook her head.

"Shut your eyes and close me out of it," directed Newcomen. "Then tell me what the big idea really is like."

She closed her eyes.

"When happiness passes a certain point, it's very like pain," she said.

"Great beauty *is* that way. It saddens us a bit," he agreed. "A fine painting. Greek sculpture. I know."

"No, you don't know. But perhaps you've had your foot on the right road, once or twice... Everything else is hurry and effort, but love is a sort of stillness, Anthony... The sun goes out at midday; the stars begin to shine; and all the rays of them go through your heart... The pain is so great that you have to do something about it, and you smile."

She smiled, with her eyes still closed. Then she looked at Newcomen. He had locked his hands together and was staring past her at his own thoughts, which were so obscure.

At last he said: "Well, I'll confess that I don't know anything about that... You could tell that I didn't know, eh?"

"A lot of people never know about it. A lot of good fathers and mothers, even. A lot of our fine, sturdy, forthright forebears, for instance. They make fine presidents of banks and other things, but they never see the stars at noonday."

She laughed a little.

"I'm so far from it that it makes you laugh, eh?" asked Newcomen through his teeth.

"You don't want me to cry about you, Anthony, do you?"

"Oh, come!" said Newcomen.

"I could, though," said the girl.

THE MARCHESE LUCARDO, on the day of the funeral of Thomas Decker, sat in mourning clothes in a little room with a vaulted ceiling and one small rounded window that let in a bit of dirty light. A grating of small steel bars split the room in two, and on the farther side of the grating stood Emilio, the former servant of Thomas Decker. The *marchese,* taking his ease in his chair, blew cigarette smoke toward the ceiling, with the air of an artist seeing visions; Emilio gripped the bars with both hands and pressed his face against the steel.

"You think," said he, "it is nothing to be like a dog under a whip; you think it is nothing to eat the filthy spaghetti which we eat; but I say that I cannot stand it. I cannot stand it and I will not stand it. Today I talk and tell everything."

"Suppose you talk," said the *marchese,* "who will believe you?"

Emilio parted angry lips to make his answer. He rose on tiptoe to help his voice, but by degrees his emotions ran down the scale and his heels suddenly dropped to the floor again.

"*Signor* Marchese!" gasped Emilio.

Lucardo waved a hand and smiled.

"You see, Emilio," he said, "that you are utterly in my hands. Behave as I expect you to, and you receive the money I agreed to pay; but if you grow nervous and have to talk, I may be forced to leave you to the law. Remember that you have a rope around your neck, and I am the only man in the world who can untie it."

Emilio could not speak. He could only cling to the bars with his eyes closed and sick pallor in his face. The *marchese* went on: "But if you do as I direct, everything will be well. Your name will be cleared. You will walk out of prison with more money in your pocket than you ever had before, and the law will be your friend and all the crimes of the past will be forgiven. Don't let your nerves grow too shaky. At heart, you're a brave fellow. That pretended attempt at suicide—oh, that was very good! When I heard the details, I said to myself, 'Ah, that brave Emilio!'"

"*Signor* Marchese," said the trembling voice of Emilio, "I am in your hands. But will it be long?"

The *marchese* rose.

"It will not be very long, I hope," he said. "You are the stalking horse, Emilio, and if I keep close enough behind you, the real murderer may think that he can forget trouble. He may step out into the open; and then how happy we all shall be!"

THE MORNING of the funeral, Newcomen said to Hugh Churchill: "I've looked through the post mortem report, but it's not all entirely clear to me. This medical verbiage, you know."

"I looked it up on an anatomy chart," said Churchill, "so that I understand it fairly well."

"What a comfort you are, Churchill!" said Newcomen. "I always know that you'll have the precise information. You have the talent for taking pains. Someone says that amounts to genius."

Churchill bit his lip to keep from smiling too broadly. He said: "The point is that the knife did not penetrate the heart, actually."

"No?"

"No, it simply passed close beside the heart, causing a fatal hemorrhage. That was the cause of death."

"The inward bleeding. It would kill him at once, I suppose?"

"Well, not exactly."

"Can't the doctors tell?"

"Not the ones who make the examination, at least. Then I believe that a great deal depends upon shock. If the nerve shock were very great, death would be hastened. If not, it might be lingering. A great deal would depend on the vitality of the victim, also. A very great deal, I understand. I can give you the technical terminology, also."

"When I need it, I'll ask for it. Thank you, Churchill."

"Not at all. You haven't told me your plans, you know. Whether you'll be continuing at Villa Oliviera, or breaking up here."

"I'll continue, Churchill. If strangers had the garden and the house to walk around in and call their own, they'd be having half my life under their feet. I don't want that, do I?"

"I hope not," said Churchill. "And if I may ask about my own position…?"

"There's that big south room which looks over the fountain. Would you like that? You could have the one next to it also, to hang your pictures."

"That's extremely kind," said Churchill, flushing. "It means that you're contented to keep me on?"

"Let's try it for a while and see how things work out."

"Very good! Excellent!" said Churchill.

"But concerning the matter of the notes which disappeared—the notes of Nicholas Decker and the *marchese* and Aldo Bertelli…"

"I don't know what to do about them, Churchill."

"Find the thief and it may lead to something."

"No doubt. We'll use time and the police for that."

The funeral went out the Siena road to Allori, where the body of Thomas Decker was buried in the shadow of some of the tall cypresses. Few people were there.

And as the ceremony ended, Newcomen found himself close to the side of Marchese Lucardo.

He said: "By the way, you may be interested to know that the alibi of Nicholas Decker and Aldo Bertelli isn't worth a rap."

"Well, well!" murmured the *marchese*. "Of course I'm interested. But how in the world did you happen to find out?"

"Luck—chance—that sort of thing. No phony alibi will stand up if it's enquired into. I suppose," said Newcomen.

That funeral ceremony was something to remember for the

Nancy cried out: "No! No! No!"
and sprang straight between
Newcomen and the levelled gun.

graceful gravity of the Italians who attended it and the chattering unconcern of the Americans. There was no more grief at the grave of Thomas Decker than his cynical soul could have expected. His chief heir, Anthony Newcomen, seemed concerned only about the physical comfort of the guests. He found time to chat with Nancy Ormonde.

"Why is Bertelli eyeing me?" he asked her.

"Aldo? Is he eyeing you?"

"He doesn't approve of us chatting together. You'll hear from him afterward."

"You shouldn't talk in such an odd way, Tony. I'm not responsible to Aldo, you know."

"Aren't you?" asked Newcomen. "I'm glad to know that."

"Why, Tony?"

"I don't approve of international marriages. Do you?" he asked.

"Tony, you mustn't be a boor," she said sharply.

"Bore, you mean, don't you?" asked Newcomen. "But I can't help noticing when a fellow looks at me with a duellist's eye like Bertelli's."

"Do you think he really is hating you?" asked the girl. "I mean, to the danger point?"

"Hate from a Bertelli is always dangerous," said Newcomen. "There's as much point to him as there is to a knife. Will you spend tomorrow evening with me?"

"If I do, will you keep talking like this?"

"Certainly not. I've finished."

"Then I'd like to see you tomorrow evening. What shall we do?"

"Anything we think of," said Newcomen, and left her.

LUCARDO DRIFTED near him as they were leaving the cemetery.

"I didn't offend you, back there, did I?" he asked anxiously.

"Oh, certainly not. I'm afraid that I was the abrupt one," said

Newcomen. "By the way, if I should be picked out of the Arno one of these days, or found in a corner with a bullet through my head or discovered with a knife stuck in my back, call on Bertelli and see what he's been doing, will you?"

"Do you mean that?" cried Lucardo under his breath.

"He knows that I've mopped up his alibi for midnight of the murder day," said Newcomen. "That's the only reason he could have for detesting me. And every time his eye touches me, it sharpens to a point. Now notice this: I've upset a midnight alibi, but what importance is there in that when Tom Decker was stabbed, as everybody knows, in the early morning? Why is Bertelli so desperately anxious about where he was at midnight? Don't you think there may be some meaning in that?"

"There must be a meaning," said the *marchese.* "Will you trust me to look into it?"

"With all my heart," said Newcomen.

He met Dinah Moore at his car.

"You drive," he said.

He closed her into the driver's seat, and while she was adjusting it forward he got in beside her and slipped down until the top of the cushion supported his head.

"Go out Siena way, will you?" he asked.

She took the looping road toward Siena which winds through beautiful country like music through the words of a song. Vineyards and olive groves fill the hollows, villas or little defensible towns sit up on the high places.

He offered her some red roses he was holding.

She handled the wheel with one hand; the other dexterously fastened the small red buds at her breast.

"Why is it that a man likes to see a woman do things with her hands? For instance, soft, pretty hands at a bit of sewing. Terribly pleasant to watch, aren't they?"

She said nothing.

"Or dealing with roses. That's about the best thing I know," said Newcomen. "Look at your hand, Dinah."

She lifted her hand from the wheel and looked at it.

"That's why I'm no good as a painter," she said. "I ought to have a big, strong, spreading hand. Then I could do things."

"Don't talk mind stuff; talk about living; talk about pretty hands," he urged lazily. "I could start a game of suppose. Suppose winter and the sting of cold in the air, and the hands of Dinah fastening a deep dark roll of silver fox around her throat. Or else it might be the broad, soft, full, brown, warm collar of a sable coat. Your hands would look well against sable. Or on velvet. But above all, they are charming when they touch red roses, just breaking from the bud, and quite fragrant…"

"Did you have a pleasant talk with Nancy Ormonde? You like her, I see," she said.

"Yes. She shows how nice a girl can be. She didn't say a single word about the way you and I are spending time together."

"Are other people saying a good deal?" she asked.

"This is Florence, you know. There's bound to be talk."

"I wonder what you'll gain by it?" she pondered. "Of course a girl's reputation is so unimportant these days. But what can you really gain by dropping acid for seven days on a Dinah Moore?"

"It doesn't seem possible that it could mean five thousand dollars to me, does it?" he agreed.

"No. Nor five hundred. Nor five."

"Ah, there you're wrong. In fact *this* is worth five or five hundred. Just to sit here and watch you; to sit for long, long moments and study your loveliness in profile."

"You've been reading art books, Anthony."

"It doesn't matter where I find the words, so long as I fit them together in the right places. Turn right here and take the by-road and lanes all the way back. I'll have dinner at your house this evening."

"I'm sorry. I'm going out," she said.

"Please let me have dinner with you."

"Is that a definite request?"

"Yes."

"Very well," she said shortly.

"To continue with the profile."

"I wish you wouldn't."

"If I were an inspired artist with gifted hands. I would spend most of my time on the throat and on the lines above it. Nose and mouth and chin…"

"Anthony!" said the girl, slowing the car.

"But this shouldn't annoy you. Dinah; not even as much as facing a camera."

She drew a deep breath.

"Tell me why it torments you," he insisted.

"You talk as though you were describing an angel. But I know what you really think of me."

"Ah, what *do* I think, then?"

HER LIPS pinched together and she shook her head.

"There's an automobile behind us," said Newcomen. "And if you go as slowly as this, we'll have to eat its dirt."

"It wants to go faster than the road allows. Let it pass," said Dinah Moore, and eased the heavy machine to a stop.

He dipped into the side pocket of the automobile, and pulled out a big forty-five calibre automatic pistol.

He said, quietly: "Don't engage the gears. Don't attempt to start the car suddenly. Turn off the motor."

She turned off the motor.

The whine of the car behind them grew louder and louder.

"Who's driving?" asked Newcomen. "Look in the mirror and tell me."

"I can't tell—it's a man."

The whine of the motor bore down on them like the cry of a bird on the wing. Newcomen lifted himself till one knee rested on the seat.

"It's my old friend Bertelli, I think," he said.

The second car slowed as though it were going to pause beside them, then gathered fresh impetus and shot past. Newcomen watched it, with the gun still in his hand. The driver, his head lowered, was obscured by the down-bent brim of his hat. He went by like a whiplash.

"Who was it?" asked Newcomen. "Why did he slow up as though he were going to stop and then jump away when he saw my gun? Who was it? And who were the people behind the curtains in the rear of the car?"

"I don't know," said Dinah Moore.

"It was Aldo Bertelli."

The dust cloud raised by the other car gradually sagged away down the wind.

"Is Bertelli frightfully interested in you, Dinah?" he asked. "You can start the motor again."

She started it.

"I hardly know him," she said.

"He was following *me*," said Newcomen. "What a lark that might have turned out to be! But he decided to pass on. Or *was* it Aldo, after all? But I thought for a moment that you were stopping because you wanted to speak with him—or did you think that *I* might want to have a few words with him?"

She made no answer. She was resting her elbows on the wheel with her head bowed, her eyes closed, breathing deeply. He looked at the white of her face and said nothing more. After a time she engaged the gears and started the car softly down the road.

"Do you think," she asked suddenly, "that I slowed up the car and stopped so that they could overtake us?"

"Suspect you, my dear?" said Newcomen. "Certainly not. Beautiful girls are an act of God, aren't they? So how could there be any real evil in them?"

Neither of them spoke again before they arrived at the *villino*. With one hand in his coat pocket, Newcomen was fingering the tangled threads of a silk tassel.

"I HOPE the cook will be able to find the right thing," Dinah said when they entered the *villino*.

"Is he a good cook?"

"Oh, yes. He used to work for Nancy Ormonde. And she only has good things in her house, you know. What shall I wear?"

"I don't know, exactly. Something yellow or gold perhaps. Before you go, tell me something pleasant to think about, won't you?"

"Just follow your fancy," she said.

"As far as Aldo Bertelli?" he suggested.

She looked at him curiously.

"You left the gun in the car, didn't you?" she asked.

"Yes," he nodded.

"There's a thirty-calibre automatic over there in the top drawer of that chest," she said, pointing. "I keep it oiled and loaded. You can have that for company when you start thinking about Bertelli."

He went to the drawer, picked out the gun, weighed it in his hand, and put it away inside his coat.

"I'm glad to have it," he said. "But why do you keep a loaded gun around?"

"Oh, I'm like any other girl," she said, "I'm afraid of mice—and rats!"

She went out of the room and left him standing. After a long moment he heard her singing in the room above. The sound seemed to come to him from two directions—through the floor or down the stairs, and also floating more faintly, a purer music, through the window. He sat down to watch the ending of the day, while Florence dimmed in all its outlines and then sank into the lake of stars.

Silver began to chime and glasses chinked in the adjoining dining room. He was aware that something had entered the dusky room and was watching him. When he turned his head suddenly, he saw the yellow-green eyes of Hans in a corner.

"Come here, Hans," he said.

The dog stood still.

He crossed the floor and stood over Hans. "Good fellow!" he said.

Hans showed the shining sharpness of his teeth, but Newcomen leaned and gradually extended his hand toward the head of the dog.

"I wouldn't do it," said the girl from the doorway.

"Wouldn't you?" asked Newcomen.

"He'll take off your hand at the wrist," she stated.

"Will he?" said Newcomen.

He laid his hand on the head of the dog. Hans shuddered violently. Long, sticky drops of slaver drooled from his mouth. Newcomen, by careful degrees, removed his hand again.

"Are you sweating?" asked the girl.

"A bit," he answered. "Hans scares me a little."

"But it feeds you, doesn't it?" she went on, entering the room.

"What feeds me, Dinah?"

"Danger. You taste it bit by bit. You relish it like a wine-taster."

"I relish your dress, Dinah. Bit by bit. Like a wine-taster. I'll think better of myself to the end of my days for knowing that yellow would look well on you."

"Dinner's ready," she said. "Shall we go in?"

They went into the dining room.

A black cat, narrow as a weasel and sleek as satin, arched its back and rubbed against the dress of Dinah.

"A cat too?" he said. "I hadn't seen the cat before."

"She keeps close to the smell of food," said Dinah as they sat down. "Hans pretends not to notice food, and steals it when your back is turned if it happens to be to his taste. He's frightfully particular, though. Hans is a purist, when it comes to food. But Esther—that's her name—makes herself beautiful and begs."

THUNDER BANGED a drum right over the house. A damp, cool wind that had been rising, suddenly carried an uproar of rain against the side of the house, and the dining-room curtains streamed out like flags.

The maid, serving the fish, had her hands full. Dinah and Newcomen ran to close the windows. The uproar of the storm was deafening. The panes rattled like snare drums sounding a charge.

"Just a little Italian surprise, eh?" asked Newcomen, as they stood for a moment together, watching the dark fingers of the rain at work.

"No, I smelled it coming," said Dinah Moore.

"You can't do that, can you?"

"Yes. Like a *contadina.*"

"Is there any Italian in you, Dinah?"

"You know how I happened to meet Tom, don't you? I wanted to see the house my great-grandmother came from."

"Italo-Spanish?" he asked.

"And Irish and English," she answered. "Anthony, did you really think, out there on the road, that I was driving you into a trap?"

He answered: "I don't think so now. Was I rather sour?"

"Not at all. You were only brisk and firm."

She cried out suddenly: "Hans!"

The big dog had put his forefeet on her chair and was sniffing her plate. He shrank instantly into the shadows on the floor.

"You see the sort of thief he is?" asked the girl, as she sat down.

"He came to the point, but he didn't steal, though," said Newcomen.

"There's some fear of the law in him, then," she agreed, beginning on the fish.

"Wait a minute," said Newcomen. She made a pause, watching him.

He got so far into his thoughts that he forgot the dinner and lighted a cigarette.

"That big devil Hans was up there long enough to steal your fish three times over," he said through the smoke.

"It's fear of the law, Anthony," she repeated.

"There's no more law in him than there is in his father the wolf," answered Newcomen.

"What are you thinking of?" asked the girl.

"There are more things than stilettos in Italy," he said. "Do you mind if I try something?"

"Of course not."

"Give me your plate, then."

She looked at him for a moment and then passed the plate across the table. Newcomen picked up Esther and offered her a bit of the fish, mincing the white sauce into it. Esther began to purr. She closed her eyes as she started on that delicacy, but after she had swallowed a few morsels she lifted her head and remained at stiff attention, as though she heard out of the distance some sound of danger which was inaudible to their human ears.

Dinah Moore said, whispering: "Anthony, what do you think?"

He put Esther back on the floor.

"Offer some of *my* portion to Hans," said Newcomen gruffly, passing his plate across the table.

She stared at him for a moment and then lowered the plate toward the dog. Hans hesitated only to make sure, by sniffing the hand of his mistress, that this miracle actually was taking place, then he wolfed down the fish.

"It wasn't the law that he was afraid of," said Newcomen.

Something howled from a corner of the room, a cry with both human and devil in it. Esther streaked over the floor and ran up a curtain to the window-rod above. On that narrow footing she turned with her hair bristling, her tail as big as a club, her dainty little ears flattened, and showed the full gape of her pink mouth at some invisible enemy. She struck with a forepaw at the empty air and then dropped sidelong to the floor.

Dinah Moore was already up and running to the place. But Newcomen went back into the pantry.

"Where's the cook?" he asked of the maid.

"He's gone out into the cool for a moment, *signore*. He loves the open air after the rain has washed it. Does *signore* wish something?" said the maid.

"Call him in," commanded Newcomen.

He waited in the pantry. Presently he could hear the voice of the woman calling: "Roberto! Roberto! Oh, Roberto!"

After that he returned to the dining room.

The girl sat by the wall with the loose, black satin of Esther's body across her lap. She supported the head with one hand and with the other stroked the delicacy of the fur.

"Well?" asked Newcomen.

She did not lift her head, and from the downward angle of her face he barely could make out that the faintest of smiles was on her lips. She seemed to be in the midst of a daydream.

Outside the house, the voice of the maid still called for Roberto; she had commenced to shriek out the name.

MARCHESE LUCARDO, on the afternoon of Thomas Decker's funeral, instead of returning to his own house stopped off at the Villa Oliviera and had Lorenzo, the butler, show him into the big study. Lorenzo went off about his duties, while Lucardo sat down to a cigarette with full leisure, for he was the most unhurried man in the world. After a time he rose, put a chair in place beside the telephone on the desk, and stood back to regard it; finally he got down on his fat knees and commenced to search the floor.

The afternoon light left the tiles in thick watery shadow, which he penetrated with a small pocket torch. He found nothing, and sat down cross-legged to contemplate his failure and another cigarette, but the preconception which brought him to the studio was so great that presently he began the search again, lying almost flat so that his eye could scan the floor at a more acute angle.

He saw something at last that got him to his knees.

It was a line a few inches long, ruled straight, and composed of very small dots, as of liquid drops which had dried. Lucardo moistened the tip of his forefinger and rubbed one of those tiny spots away. It left on the skin a little streak of brownish red which he studied for a moment with the greatest interest. Afterward, he rubbed his finger clean on a scrap of paper, folded the paper, and slipped it into a vest pocket.

A warmth of tender geniality kept Lucardo smiling as he drove back into Florence and left at the office of the commissary of police that small fold of paper. "See if the streak on it is blood," he said, "and identify the type of blood."

The commissary showed the greatest interest. "What have you found. Franco?" he asked. "Where has that wise nose of yours been sniffing?"

"It's the blood of Thomas Decker," said Lucardo, "taken off the studio floor. If that's true, he was stabbed in the house and only went into the garden to die."

"Stabbed in the house?" cried the commissary. "Stabbed in the studio through the heart, and then he walks calmly out into the garden?"

"Stabbed *near* the heart, not through it," said Lucardo, "and one thin flicker of blood came off the stiletto and fell on the floor. The shock of the stroke might very well have dropped Decker as though he were clubbed over the head; and that would satisfy the murderer. Afterward, recovering his consciousness in part, Decker feels no pain. He only knows that he wants air. He hurries out into the open…"

"But if that is true," said the commissary, "then Emilio's confession…"

"Is good enough to put the murderer at ease," answered Lucardo. "When you find out the type of this blood, telephone to Decker's doctor and find out the type of *his* blood. If the two are the same, it is almost certain that Decker was stabbed in the studio; Emilio and the American, Newcomen, must be innocent; and several other people may be suspected."

"Ah, Franco, what a happiness is in your face! Some day I am going to write a book and tell the world all the truth about you."

"My dear friend," said the *marchese*, "do you want to end all my usefulness at a stroke? Only a fool is able to walk through every door and be welcome."

HUGH CHURCHILL, on the evening of that day, reached the villa of Marchese Lucardo while the sun was still in the sky and was told that the *marchese* could see no one.

"He is occupied in the *podere, signore*," said the butler.

But privacy was not a thing that Churchill respected in the lives of others. He had a feeling that business at all costs came first, in all things; so he wandered down the paths of the Lucardo farm, among the olive trees and the grape vines until he found the *marchese* sitting on a stone with his hands folded over the top of a walking stick.

"Ah, Mr. Churchill," said the *marchese*, rising. "It is a pleasure. Take this stone and sit down."

"I have only a moment. It is warm," said Churchill, wiping his face with a handkerchief.

"It is warm," said the *marchese*, "but I'm in the habit of spending a time at the end of each day down here."

"Every day?" asked Churchill, staring.

"No, only when I have large problems to solve."

"I came to see you particularly about one thing, *marchese.*"

"Tell me, then," said Lucardo.

"It is about Mr. Newcomen."

"An interesting man."

"Tony is quite a boy," said Churchill carelessly. "And he is apt to make trouble for you."

"I'm sorry to hear that."

"Unless he is prevented," said Churchill.

"Do tell me how to prevent him, then," said Lucardo. He lifted his head and fixed his gentle eye upon the secretary.

"The thing is this," said Churchill. "He has found out that the notes which you and Nicholas Decker and Aldo Bertelli left in the hands of Thomas Decker have disappeared from the safe."

"Well, well!" murmured the *marchese.*

"But he has not yet discovered," said Churchill, "the letter which Thomas Decker wrote to you the day before he died, demanding immediate payment of that note."

SINCE THE letter was written to me," said Lucardo, "is it strange that he has not found it?"

"The carbon copy is what I speak of," said Churchill, stepping back a little to study the expression of the *marchese* more carefully. "To fill out his file, Mr. Decker always used to sign his carbons. He did so at my request. I feel that it makes the records more emphatic in a legal sense."

"Oh, no doubt."

"But if he finds the carbon of the letter and realizes the strength with which Mr. Decker expressed himself to you about the payment of the debt—the day before the murder—do you think that Mr. Newcomen might draw a few deductions?"

"Let me see. I wonder!" murmured Lucardo. "Do you think he

would suspect me of having killed Tom Decker? Not that, Mr. Churchill!"

"How can I tell?" asked Churchill. "Another thing that I call to your attention—it is known that you were at the Villa Oliviera just before midnight of the fatal day, *marchese*."

"It is known?" asked Lucardo, lifting his brows so that his whole face seemed to lengthen.

"It is known to one person," said Churchill.

"You surprise me very much," said the *marchese*. "I'm sure that if anyone knew, he would have started an ugly rumor circulating."

"No doubt you *would* think so," said Churchill. He stepped closer and said in a soft voice: "But some men are born with discretion in their blood."

"No doubt," said Lucardo.

"A little money would put the carbon copy of the letter in your hand and silence the voice that might speak against you, *marchese*," remarked Churchill.

"Would it?" asked Lucardo. "That would be worthwhile. How much would it cost, Mr. Churchill?"

"Just a few thousand dollars. Say five thousand?"

"Five thousand? It does not seem a very great deal. But put it in lire."

Churchill's lips twisted, so great was his scorn for a man without the ability to perform simple feats of arithmetic.

"Say ninety thousand lire," he suggested.

"Ninety thousand lire! But that is a fortune, Mr. Churchill. And, as you know, I am a poor man."

"Bertelli is poor. So is Nicholas Decker. But among the three of you, you ought to be able to raise that much," declared Churchill.

"Bertelli? Decker?" echoed the *marchese,* with a blank face.

"In short," said Churchill, "I saw with my own eyes at different times all three of you at the Villa Oliviera just before midnight. Sneaking in a furtive way through the garden."

The *marchese* stared at him.

"At this moment," said Churchill, "there is a police rumor out that Decker was stabbed at midnight in his studio."

"Is it possible?" cried Lucardo.

"The three of you can raise that much money," insisted Churchill. "I'll make it a round sum. So that you can remember it. Say sixty thousand lire. You understand me?"

"I try to," said the *marchese.*

Churchill drew from his pocket a fold of paper and slapped his hand with it.

"Try harder," he suggested in his dry voice. "Get the other two to help you think it out. Otherwise, the three of you go to jail! I can show the motives. I can prove that you were all at the Villa Oliviera at about the time of the crime."

"Is it true?" asked Lucardo. "Do we have to pay all of this money? What you know about me is clear, but what do you know about the others? How shall I persuade them to help me raise the money?"

"Persuade them?" laughed Churchill. Pleasure made him strike his hands together. "Listen to me and I'll give you guns to hold under their noses."

THE MARCHESE LUCARDO met Bertelli and Nicholas Decker at Doney's, which stands on the Via Turnaboundi as a Gossip Exchange where elements of the foreign colony meet with Italians for cocktails and the interchange of news. The cellar is good, the drinks are not very expensive and an air of not too moldering age clings to the place, so that even the best people are led easily into the conversational murders of casual talk.

"I have come to you for help," said the *marchese.*

"For help? You?" asked Bertelli, lifting his handsome face suddenly from his thoughts. Then, as he studied the *marchese,* a smile pulled at a corner of his mouth but was mastered instantly.

"But you can't need help," said Nicholas Decker. "A man with your position with the police is able to make trouble for others. Who can touch you, Franco?"

The *marchese* sighed. Then he answered: "The truth is that I was seen late the other evening at the Villa Oliviera. It was the evening, you know, when Decker was murdered."

"Evening?" exclaimed Bertelli. "Not at all. It was about dawn when Decker was stabbed in the back in the garden of the Oliviera."

"So we all thought," nodded Lucardo. "But ah, the police are such clever devils! They have found on the floor of the study at the Oliviera a little streak a few inches long where drops of something sprayed on the tiles. A thing almost impossible to see, but those clever foxes see everything. What people, my dear friends, what dangerous wolves these police are!"

"But what was it?" demanded Nicholas Decker.

"It was blood of the same type as that of Thomas Decker. It proves that he was stabbed while he was in the studio. Therefore, the blow was struck at about midnight," explained Lucardo with a sigh. "And I, unfortunately, was seen near the villa at about that hour by Churchill."

"That man is a buzzard," said Nicholas Decker. "Whenever he appears, I think of dead things."

"Suppose you *were* seen late at the Villa Oliviera," said Bertelli. "Does that connect you with the killing of Decker, poor Franco?"

"*You* would not believe such a thing of me, Aldo, I know," said the gratified *marchese*.

Bertelli laughed.

"No, I would hardly believe that," he answered.

"Motives—motives—motives," said Nicholas Decker. "A good detective finds the motive first and afterward he does something about the criminal. What earthly motive could you have, Franco?"

"Well," murmured Lucardo, "it seems that I owed money to

Decker. Not a great sum in dollars. But there is always the trouble when one translates dollars into lire. They become twenty times as much. And that is a pity!"

The simplicity of this remark caused the two guests of the *marchese* to look at one another and then to laugh.

Bertelli said: "If I were you, I would pay no attention to the matter."

"The fact is, however," continued Lucardo, "that only the day before poor Decker died, he sent me a very crisp letter demanding payment of the sum I owed him. A very stern letter. It troubled me so much that I went over my accounts; but I found no money in them. Then I went to my bank, and I found no money there, either."

"You might have guessed that by looking at your bank book, perhaps," suggested Bertelli, yawning a little.

"True," said Lucardo. "But whenever I think of the bank and the amount of money locked up in it, it seems a pity if a man cannot talk a little of the gold out of its vaults. I always go in hope. It was so the other day, and I had to come away without a penny. So I went up late that evening on the chance that I might be able to see Decker. I did, as a matter of fact, see him."

"Ah, you did?" exclaimed Nicholas Decker. "At what time?"

"Let me see. Was it eleven-thirty? Yes, it was about that hour. I talked very earnestly with Decker. I talked and told him the truth, and at length he did a strange thing. A very strange thing."

"Well?" queried Bertelli, who kept his head high and his dark eyes keenly attentive, now.

"Decker was a close-fisted man," said Lucardo. "It seemed hard for him to let go of his money."

Bertelli snapped: "He never gave a penny except when he expected a big return. Go on, Franco."

"The amazing thing was that on that night Decker suddenly took from his pocket the very note which I had signed and gave it back to me," said the *marchese,* shaking his head in such wonder that his fat cheeks quivered a little.

"GAVE IT back to you?" echoed Bertelli, bewildered.

"He gave it back," said Lucardo, "and he also shook me very warmly by the hand and told me to think no more about it. His words are still in my ears. They were warm, cordial words. He said: 'What are old friends for except to be useful to one another? What are we worth if we only give one another pain? Forget the letter I wrote to you. Only remember that bad humor grips all of us like gout, now and then, and causes us to do things which we regret.' With those words, he gave me the note, as I say, and a moment later I left. It was an unusual act for Decker, I think."

"Very unusual," said Bertelli. "It never would have happened unless he had been in a pinch and thought he might need help."

"My help? But what could I do for such a rich man?" asked Lucardo, opening his innocent eyes.

"You have the whole of the police at your beck and call—though heaven knows how you manage it," said Nicholas Decker.

"For services rendered," commented Bertelli, making little effort to disguise his irony. "Franco gets no more from the police than he gives them."

"You think," said Lucardo, "that Decker expected to be in need of police help, even before he was killed?"

"It sounds that way," answered Nicholas Decker. "But why do you need our help, now?"

"The added point," said Lucardo, "is that it seems that there is a file of Decker's correspondence, and Decker's letter to me demanding payment was produced by the secretary, Churchill, yesterday. He suggested that if he showed the letter to the police they would be interested. It supplied the motive for a crime, do you see? And Churchill himself saw me at the villa—at what you might call a guilty hour. The secretary wanted five thousand dollars for the letter. What do you think?"

"A great deal of money!" breathed Nicholas Decker with a broad, two-handed gesture.

But Bertelli, his face dark with thought, answered: "I'd find that money if I could, Franco. I'd find it and pay it, if I were you, and then burn that letter. Not that they could hang you on such evidence, but it would do your reputation more than five thousand dollars worth of harm."

"Hugh Churchill seemed to think so," agreed the *marchese* sadly. "But I simply have not the money. When I told Churchill that, he suggested that I call on you two. He thought you would be interested in helping me to pay."

"We? Interested?" exclaimed Nicholas Decker, half rising from his chair. He looked wildly toward Bertelli, and was met by a terrible glance of disapproval that deflated him, as it were, and caused him to slip down into his chair again. "Why should we be interested?"

"As old friends, of course," said Bertelli steadily. "What else did this Churchill have to say?"

"Nothing else of any great importance," said Lucardo. "But now you know why I have called you together today. It was simply in wonder, my friends, whether or not you could help me."

"Impossible!" said Nicholas Decker.

"Absolutely impossible," said Bertelli. "This is your own affair, after all, and not ours. Even Churchill cannot connect us!"

"Ah, Aldo, and my dear Nicholas, it appears that there you are wrong. Churchill has ugly things to report about you both."

"Has he?" asked Bertelli. "Suppose you begin with me. For what earthly reason should there have been bad blood between me and the American?"

"It is a strange little story," said Lucardo. "We know that *Signor* Decker went constantly through the country looking at pictures in little churches and in small private collections. He found some good things that way, and used to buy them very cheaply, but when his name became known as a collector, people recognized him and doubled or quadrupled their asked prices. So he got in the habit of spotting what he wanted and then sending other people to bargain for him. So it appears that he found a picture in Prato, a picture with a dirty face which was nevertheless a real Gaddi and worth a fortune. It could be bought for a few hundred lire, but only by an unknown. So he sent you to buy the picture, Aldo. Isn't that true?"

BERTELLI SAID nothing. He kept his bright, grim eyes fixed on Lucardo, shifting the glance slowly up and down as though he were reading a page.

"But it seems you discovered that the great American house of Laubenheimer and Fitzroy were interested enormously in having a Gaddi picture and they would pay a very high price; so you managed to forget Thomas Decker and sold the Gaddi directly to—"

"That's enough!" snapped Bertelli.

"But is it true?" said Nicholas Decker. He leaned back in his chair and laughed. "How Tom must have ground his teeth and cursed! A Gaddi? Tadeo?"

"Yes," nodded Lucardo. "I'm afraid that it was, although it's still on the way to America and hasn't been finally experted there."

"Did Offner see it before it went?" asked Nicholas Decker.

"Yes," nodded Lucardo. "He said it was real."

"Then it *was* the real thing," nodded Nicholas Decker. "And no wonder there was bad blood between Aldo and Tom. But all this has nothing to do with me, as you can see for yourself. There's no reason why Churchill should expect me to help you raise money, Franco."

"There's the pity of it," said Lucardo. "He has dug up even worse evidence against you, Niccolo. He says that the very day before the killing of Decker you called at the villa and got into a terrible rage because he would not advance you any more money."

"He lies!" said Nicholas Decker, but fear had choked his voice to a whisper.

"… and that you shouted at Thomas Decker that if he disgraced you and let you go bankrupt, you'd put a knife in him."

"A knife?" said Bertelli, lifting his handsome narrow face.

"A lie!" said Nicholas Decker. He leaned back in his chair with a white face and trembling lips.

"No. We must put our heads together," said Bertelli. *"Something always can be done."*

"Do you think so?" asked Lucardo with gratitude.

Nicholas Decker was about to break in again, but a flick of the eye of Bertelli, sharp as the snap of a whiplash, silenced him.

"We ought first of all," said Bertelli, "to find out what exactly is in the mind of Churchill."

"I've told you as nearly as I can," said Lucardo. "Money seems to be what he has in mind."

"Exactly," said Bertelli dryly. "But suppose we find out just where our friend Churchill was when he saw you come into the villa, that night?"

"Do you mean from what place he saw me?" asked Lucardo.

"I mean exactly that," said Bertelli.

"He did not confide in me," answered Lucardo.

"Perhaps not. Couldn't you draw it from him?" snapped Bertelli.

"It didn't occur to me to dwell on the point," said Lucardo. "Should I have done so?"

Bertelli drew a short, quick breath.

"You failed to do so. That ends it," he asserted.

An idea struck Nicholas Decker and made him swallow his cocktail suddenly.

"The sneaking ferret—he has a face like a ferret, that Churchill—

he may have been hanging about in the garden of the place the entire evening."

"Or looking out windows, perhaps," suggested Lucardo.

"Confound it, man," snapped Decker, "there's no window that looks down on the entrance to the studio at the Villa Oliviera."

"Isn't there?" asked Lucardo innocently. "Ah, now that I think of it, I believe you're right."

"He believes that I'm right," said Nicholas Decker with some sort of fierce irony in his voice. "This rat-hole peeker of a Churchill; this eavesdropper, this...."

"Well?" said Bertelli, lifting his eyebrows a little.

"But the money?" asked Lucardo with a gentle insistence. "Are you going to be able to help me?"

IT WAS as a result of this conversation that Hugh Churchill, early in the afternoon, received a telephone call from Lucardo, who said: "Concerning the five thousand dollars—"

"Not over the telephone, man!" cried Churchill.

"I saw Bertelli and Nicholas Decker and told them that you had suggested their names."

"Told them that I had suggested their names?"

"Ah, but you did, didn't you?"

"*Signor* Marchese, I'll see you wherever you please, but don't telephone about—"

"Unhappily, my news is all too brief," said the *marchese*. "They could not let me have a penny, to their own great regret, they said. And so I cannot possibly raise the money you require."

Churchill slammed up the telephone.

He hardly dared look about him for a moment, until he realized that if the conversation had been overheard it could only have been through the wire and not by any casual eavesdropper in the room. As his fear left him, a more vital anger took its place.

He hurried to the small room where the complicated files of

the villa were kept, and, taking a paper out of a drawer, he went straight to find Newcomen in the library.

Churchill came in with a militant air and a straight back.

He said: "I never mentioned having seen the Marchese Lucardo in the garden at nearly twelve o'clock on the night of the murder. It never occurred to me that his presence might be significant until I was running through the file, just now, and discovered this letter. It may interest you."

He put it in the hand of Newcomen, unfolded. It read:

My dear Franco,

I have let the note run overdue for a long time. Sixty-five hundred dollars is not a fortune. But we grow no younger and money is no easier to come by.

If your son keeps on spending at the present rate, you soon will have nothing left of your estate. I put in this claim before the moneylenders clean you out.

I have to insist on immediate payment. If merely writing you letters is no good, then I'll have to go to law.

And perhaps you realize sufficiently well that the instant one suit against you commences, a dozen other claimants will rush to the courts.

Consult your own good sense, and make the payment to me at once.

       Yours sincerely,

         Thomas Decker.

IN THE late afternoon of the third day after the murder of Thomas Decker, Newcomen smoked a pipe in the chapel and watched in silence while Dinah Moore worked at the restoration of the fresco. When she finished, he walked down the hill with her to the *villino*. In three hours she had not spoken three words. Sometimes she had taken her eyes from her work to look at him, but with no meaning in her face except the blank concentration which appears in those who are seeing only with the eye of the mind. Even when she went down the slope over the terraces with him, the preoccupation still held her until she came to the Hercules level. There she stopped, looked up and down the water-lily canal, and then continued down to the wall that fenced the place from the road. She went over the wall like a boy and jumped to the ground below. The dog sprang behind her, and Newcomen, from above, regarded them both with a keen attention before he followed. He landed with the lightness of an athlete in spite of his bulk.

"What have you just learned, Anthony?" she asked.

He merely smiled.

"I saw your eyes open and swallow quite a big fish," she said.

Instead of answering he said: "Tell me, Dinah; are you going to do nothing about that Roberto—that kitchen poisoner of yours?"

"Why should I do anything?" she asked.

"You're not even going to inform the police?"

"They'd only put him in prison for life," she replied.

"Wouldn't that be a gain?"

"Not for me. I'd like to know who hired him. That's all."

"Are you sure that he was paid to do it?"

"Yes. Perhaps not in cash, but it was not his own idea. He'd been spying on me for a long time."

"Why did you keep him, then? Do you like trouble for its own sake?"

"No, I'm not like you, Anthony. I thought that perhaps, sooner or later, I might be able to discover the person behind him, if I kept him in the house long enough. But I failed. That's all."

"What was the poison?"

"I don't know."

"I told you to have a post-mortem performed on the cat."

"I know you told me," she admitted.

"You didn't do it?"

"No."

"Tell me where it is buried. I'll attend to it," said Newcomen.

She said nothing.

"Tell me, Dinah," he insisted.

"No," she said firmly, with the air of one who has thought a thing out to the end.

"If an investigation starts, are you afraid of what it might lead to?" he asked suddenly.

They had reached the front loggia of her house and she stopped short and stared at him. Then, silently, she went on to the door. He followed behind her.

With her hand on the door knob, without looking back at him, she said in a low, rapid voice: "I wish you would let me be alone this evening."

"My last remark was a little thick, eh?" he asked.

"Yes," she said, and pushed the door open. "Good night, Anthony."

But he walked in behind her. In the dimness of the hall they faced one another. He would have given a good deal for a clearer view of her, but after a moment, without speaking, she went on into the living room. It was never a very brilliant apartment. A climbing vine clouded one window with green, and a great oleander, now brilliant with pink bloom, stood close to the other.

He said: "If they find the cook, they'll find out why you hired him. If you accuse him of attempted murder, of what will he accuse you?"

The telephone rang in the corner of the room. She went to it.

"Yes," she said. "I'll see."

SHE COVERED the mouthpiece with the flat of her hand.

"Are you here?" she asked. "I think it's Nancy Ormonde who wants to speak to you."

He went over to the phone and took it from her.

"Hello," he said.

"Oh, Tony," said the weary voice of Nancy Ormonde. "When you weren't at the villa, I guessed where I might find you, of course. You don't mind me ringing you there, do you?"

"Not a bit," he said.

"About this evening. I'm sick about not seeing you, but I have a really frightful headache. I mean, when I try to sit up the room spins. You know?"

"Are you lying down?" he asked.

"Flat. Do forgive me, Tony."

"Of course," he said. "Have you heard the news?"

"What news? News Florentine or real news?"

"Real news. Dinah's cook tried to poison her, last night."

"Tony!"

"No wonder you wouldn't keep Roberto to yourself. Did you know anything about his special talents?"

"What are you talking about?"

"It's true. I saw the cat die of the fish. Ugly thing to see."

"How horrible!" cried Nancy. "I hope it's a clear case! I hope that the police—"

"Dinah won't have the police. Queer that she won't, eh? But then she's a strange girl. Ever notice that?"

"Of course I have. Almost... Well, I won't say it. You mean that she hasn't turned the case over to the police?"

"Not a bit."

"She hasn't even tried to find out where the cook's gone?"

"She hasn't even lifted a finger."

The clearness passed out of the voice of Nancy and left the mournful drone of the sick-bed.

"It sounds too preposterous," she said. "You will forgive me for this evening, Tony?"

"Don't think about it," he answered.

"So good of you. Will you try me another time?"

"Shall we make it tomorrow?"

"That would be perfect."

"Good night, Nancy. I'll be up for you in the evening."

He rang off. When he turned, he saw Dinah Moore in the act of sitting down again in the chair by the window.

"Is that how you tell the police?" she asked.

"It's a good way, isn't it?" said Newcomen.

"It's a Florentine way," she said. "Why not stay and have supper with me?"

"You have no cook now. Don't forget that."

"The maid cooks very well."

"Besides, you want to get rid of me, this evening."

"Not now," she said.

"Are you afraid to stay alone?" he asked.

"Yes," she said.

"You hesitated before you said that," remarked Newcomen.

"Please stay," said the girl.

"Being persuaded is a charm, when you do the persuading, Dinah. It's your outright manner that pleases me most. The good, free, ardent, hearty way in which you tell your stories. That's the artist in you."

"I'm not acting, really."

"No? You simply want me here?"

She fell into one of her silences.

"Won't you persuade any more, Dinah?" he asked.

"No. I see that you're going," she said.

WHEN HE was outside the front door, Newcomen stood for a moment breathing the night, with his eyes half-closed because he wanted to go back into the house so much. Something made a scraping sound just before him, and he looked up as a man slithered down one of the pillars of the portico.

"Who's that?" asked Newcomen, and jumped for the fellow as he spoke.

The tips of his fingers brushed a shoulder as the man dodged to the side and ran back along the wall of the house. He made a tall slender silhouette and he ran like an athlete, but Newcomen was overtaking him at every step when he whipped about and fired. The bullet went by the face of Newcomen like a trailing wing-tip over his cheek. The shock stopped him for an instant. When he started again, the fugitive was around the rear corner of the villa.

When Newcomen got there, he had no sight or sound of the man to guide him. The brush came up close to the place at this point, and grass softened the ground.

Anger made Newcomen bigger as stood there, for a moment, straining his ears; then he went back to the front of the house. Dinah Moore stood under the portico.

"Anthony, are you hurt?" she asked.

He stood over her, panting. She lifted her face and kept looking at him; her hands were held out toward him, an incompleted gesture.

"Who was it?" he asked.

"I don't know. I heard the shot," she said.

"You don't know? You don't know he was up there in your room? You didn't have any *special* reason for wanting to keep me here tonight?"

"Anthony, what do you mean?" she asked. "In my room? Was someone..."

"You don't know anything, of course. It's best not to know anything," said Newcomen slowly. "And you'd always do what's best."

He turned on his heel and left her.

After a while, he got hold of himself and took his automobile straight across the city and out to the hill of Nancy Ormonde. It stood out, by night, in a strange little black pattern of trees and roof against the stars.

He did not go directly to the villa but, instead, ran his car into the mouth of a lane below it and then went up by foot and scaled the garden wall rather than walk in through the driveway. After a good old Florentine custom, broken fragments of bottle-glass, embedded in the top cement of the wall to discourage thieves, made him work with care. He was in a sweat before he dropped to the deep, soft garden soil. He paused there to eradicate the impression made by his feet. Then he stepped out on the narrow path that wound up to the villa.

Part of what he came for met him on the way. The piano strings gave into the distance only a vague rapid thrumming without resonance, but the pure soprano of a woman's voice, flawless and effortless, sang at his ear, made small but not obscure. When he reached the circle of the driveway in front of the entrance, he saw a small Italian car parked there; it was by no means the sort of an automobile that Nancy would keep for herself.

The singing came from the curtained salon, but a little V-shaped gap toward the top offered a view of the interior and the window-bars to keep out robbers presented him with a ladder for climbing. He stood close to the wall for a moment to study the garden shadows, afterward he mounted the bars until he could look through the gap between the curtains.

He saw only the red of the tiles at first, with the watery images of furniture slipping over them, but when he looked to the side, the cone of his vision embraced the piano with Nancy at the keys. She was no longer singing, but she played a gay old Neapolitan song with such force that Newcomen could not make out the words which Aldo Bertelli was pouring out with great vehemence. Bertelli stood behind her, talking with voluble gestures to the back of her bright head. Although she could not see him, it was impossible for him to abandon gestures. Now and then he paused with his hands extended, still reaching after his thought. In these intervals the girl, never turning, sometimes nodded, but as a rule she shook her head, and these denials increased the excitement of Bertelli.

He began to walk up and down the room with short turns, still exclaiming, until Nancy commenced to sing once more, her head back, smiling out the high notes with the care of an opera star. This flood of music reduced Bertelli to a silence in which he gripped his fists, ground his teeth, and stared impotently at the ceiling for a moment before he became more politely resigned.

NEWCOMEN CLIMBED down from his perch and retreated into the darkness of the garden. He was heading toward a big cypress when an obscure form moved straight at him out of the shadows. A ray of starlight glinted on something that might have been metal. Newcomen sprang with extended hands and gripped his man by the wrists.

They were rather fleshy wrists but with big bones under the fat, and Newcomen's grasp was broken by a sudden powerful movement. Like a boxer he clinched, and then heard the voice of Marchese Lucardo say quietly: "Be still, Newcomen. We don't want enough noise to bring out the servants, do we?"

Newcomen stepped back. When he had his breath under control, he said: "How long have you been here, *marchese?*"

"I? Why, I've just this moment arrived," said Lucardo.

"You generally cut in through the garden this way?" asked Newcomen. "Extraordinary fellow. You can even see in the dark."

"I?" exclaimed Lucardo, carefully keeping his voice low.

"Exactly. Otherwise, how could you know me in the dark?"

"Why, I knew you by a certain bigness you have around the shoulders and head; and I saw you against the glinting of a light from the house."

"Ah, very well," said Newcomen. "Also, you saw me against the light of that window, didn't you?"

"Which window, my dear friend?"

"Never mind," answered Newcomen. "I love a man who never says more than he has to. I won't ask you what else you have found at Nancy Ormonde's villa besides the view?"

"I don't understand," said the *marchese*.

"Naturally you wouldn't... That's Bertelli's car, by the way."

"Ah? Aldo Bertelli? Interesting."

"Very. She had a sick headache for the rest of the world, but she has songs for Aldo Bertelli. Perhaps you can fit that into your jigsaw puzzle in some way?"

"Into my what?" asked the *marchese* politely.

"Into the picture of your jigsaw puzzle," repeated Newcomen. "It may be one of the hard bits. Part of the blue of the sky, for instance... He's arguing with her very hard, and she doesn't agree with him entirely. In fact, he's rather hot under the collar. That's some more free information, which I hope that you can use."

"I am afraid I do not understand."

"Of course not," said Newcomen. "Good night."

"Good night, Mr. Newcomen."

Newcomen went out into the road by the same course he had used in entering, and, waiting for a moment in the shrubbery, he heard a motor and then a pair of headlights swept by him, and the body of Lucardo's old-fashioned, high-shouldered car.

Still Newcomen waited by the road and at last another motor came whizzing by him, honking noisily for the sharp bends in the way. He recognized the tinny little car of Bertelli.

After that, he went back to his own automobile and drove straight up to the door of Nancy Ormonde's villa.

The butler opened the door for him.

"The *signorina* is indisposed," he said.

"I know she is," answered Newcomen. "Take up a note to her, will you?" He scribbled on the back of an envelope:

Dear Nancy, I happened to be passing this way and wanted to find out how you are. Are you well enough to chat for a few moments?

Anthony.

The butler left him in the little salon with the garden view; without the view it was nothing but a high-shouldered vestibule.

The note which Nancy Ormonde sent back was in staggering handwriting:

Thanks... So kind... Simply dead... Forgive.

N.

He wrote under this sad message:

Dear Nancy,

I just came up to enjoy the view by night and apparently someone was enjoying it before me. I saw his car leave. Don't make me go with nothing but hills and distant city lights to remember.

Anthony.

The butler, returning after this message, announced: "The *signorina* descends at once. Will you sit in the library, *signore?*"

Newcomen walked up and down in the library, until Nancy Ormonde came down to him. She was wearing a flowing mist of white weighted down by a margin of embroidery in pastel shades.

"Of course I couldn't be rude, Anthony," she told him, "so here I am."

"How is the head now?" he asked.

"Dreadful," she said, making a gesture with both hands to frame her face.

"But doesn't getting up and walking help it a lot?" he asked.

She looked at him carefully.

"I wonder," she said.

"I haven't had dinner," he told her.

"I'll ring for something," she said.

"No, we'll go to town and get something."

"Where shall we dine?"

"We can go up to the Piazza Michelangelo."

"I'll go up and change... Shall I wear black?"

"You can't make a mistake," said Newcomen.

WHEN HE was alone, Newcomen looked farther about the room in the hope of finding tokens of Nancy Ormonde, and thought that he discovered a hint of her in the delicate blues and gold of the Chinese rug, and in the French mirror with its carved and gilded frame, and in three Chinese prints, unrolled against the wall. But something of significance, some vital key for which he was searching expectantly, avoided him. Then Nancy returned, dressed to go out. As they started off in the automobile, she said: "What you told me over the phone about poison and Dinah Moore—that wasn't a joke?"

"It killed the cat, anyway," he told her.

She considered this in silence, for a moment, and then asked: "Why did you choose that moment to tell me that grisly bit?"

"I wondered if you really were lying flat on your back in bed, as you said."

"And so...?" she asked.

"So I supplied a shock. There was no rustling of bedclothes, and no crunching of pillows. I decided that you were sitting in a chair."

"What does all that lead to, Tony?"

"It leads to an automobile and a Florentine night. You can see for yourself."

She put her head back and looked at the stars, without smiling.

"I've thought of a place to go," she said. "There's a little restaurant off in the corner of the Piazza Signoria. It's quiet there, at this time of night. And there's the tower to look at. Will that suit you?"

"When did you start going in for architecture, Nancy?"

"Florence has changed me," she said.

They slid down off the Arcetri hills and into the steaming bustle of the Florentine streets.

"You know Lucardo, don't you?" asked the girl.

"I've had to know him. He takes an amateur-police interest in the case of Tom Decker, so I see him now and then."

"Is he a fool or just a *fat* fox?"

"He looks simple enough," said Newcomen.

"He was questioning me. Only today. He wanted to know just what I had done on the night poor Tom was killed."

"What did you do, Nancy?"

"I don't see what in the world I had to do with it," she said. "I don't see why anybody should want to know. Great heavens, Tony, are they suspecting me?"

She laughed, but only a little. "I told the *marchese* just what I had done. I was in bed most of the evening but I couldn't sleep. I don't have insomnia often, but that was a bad attack. So I drove down into the town and then out through San Domenico. I suppose it was old habit that made me swing over past the Villa Oliviera, and then I saw a light in the *villino* and thought of seeing Dinah Moore. So I stopped and went in. We had a chat and I came home again."

"When was it?" asked Newcomen.

"Oh, say twelve-thirty; around there. What could that mean to Lucardo? He listened with his fat smile all the while, but I could see that he was making notes of everything I said."

"He's an amateur detective. What can you expect? Nothing!" said Newcomen.

"Perhaps that's it," she said.

"Of course that's it."

"You know what we ought to do, Anthony?" she asked.

"Well?"

"Stop this side and walk the rest of the way. Or can you find a couple of old alleys that wind up toward the Piazza?"

"I can find them," he said.

"Let's walk through. I was in them, once. And I've never forgotten."

"Romantic thrill, and all that?"

"Yes, all that."

He looked for her smile and did not find it. The black of her dress made her seem pale, and the stone-cut beauty of her face was set with resolution. He stopped the car obediently, parked it, and went on beside her. They had to give the sidewalk to a young Italian and his girl moving slowly, locked together, she with her head back on his shoulder and her face frozen with ethereal joy, he with his head bowed, brooding over her.

"That's the better way," said Newcomen.

"Better than what?" asked Nancy Ormonde.

"Better than the ways of the cold-blooded Nordics, who make it a battle of the wits. We conduct our love affairs somewhere between courtesy and sneering. Is this your alley, Nancy?"

She peered into the tall, narrow slot of darkness, and took his hand as though she were looking down from the brink of a perilous height.

"No, not this one. It's the other," she said. "There's a sort of flying buttress that keeps the buildings from falling in against one another... This one... This is the place..."

They moved down the alley.

"Jonah in the whale's throat—he must have felt like this," suggested Newcomen. "Why do you have to be so romantic, Nancy?"

HE STOPPED, looking up at a narrow wedge of building that had a pair of lights high above, like two eyes set close together.

"They wouldn't notice even a place like this," said Newcomen. "Those lovers we just passed. They don't know the moon is shining. The only stars they see are the ones they put in the sky... How do they begin?"

"I don't know," said Nancy Ormonde. "Let's get on through this darkness. It's not so pleasant after all."

"I suppose they've grown up in the same block," said Newcomen, without budging in spite of the urgency of her hand. "He's a metal worker, by the soot in his skin. One day when a glass of wine has sharpened his eye, he sees the girl—her whole soul—skyrocket!— it's heaven. And ever since, they've been entranced... Did you ever skyrocket like that, Nancy?"

"Not as far as heaven," she answered. "What's the matter with you, Tony?"

"There was too much Nancy in the wine. You know what that does to a man?"

"I don't know at all."

"I think you do. Even a small spot of Nancy makes the eye shine and the heart go faster. The brain spins and the tongue grows a little delirious. Haven't you seen those symptoms?"

"Not in you, Tony."

"You haven't stopped to look, though."

"Shall I stop?"

"Not if you're going to hurry on again."

She slowed almost to a halt.

"It's Florence and moonshine, not me," she said.

They were walking on slowly toward the building with the narrow front. Far before them a light showed the rugged stones of an arch, but hardly touched the uneven pavement.

"Are you trying to make me a little dizzy?" she asked.

He put his arm around her.

"I can't make you dizzy. I only make you shudder," he told her.

"Because I'm trembling with disbelief," she said. "Tony, aren't you a dreadful liar?"

"Men of twenty-five never lie," said he.

"Do you think you have inside your arm something that could make you happy, Tony?"

"What's that in the window?" exclaimed Newcomen, suddenly interrupting.

For they were by the narrow building now, and out of the black emptiness of a window he saw an obscure form emerging only three or four steps from him. The outline was so dark that it might have been man or woman, but the automatic, reaching out into the alley, was visible by its own light, as it were. It was hardly three steps from them.

Nancy cried out: "No! No, no!" and sprang straight between Newcomen and that leveled gun. The muzzle of it jerked up as it exploded. Something hit the wall behind Newcomen's head like a fist smashing its bone. The figure in the window faded as he pushed Nancy aside and leaped in through the open square of blackness.

Landing on hands and knees, his shoulder struck a chair and sent it skidding and screeching across the floor. A lock turned in a door, the rusty metal groaning.

Then, as he stood up, he heard Nancy crying softly behind him. "Come out, Tony. Come out, or I'll die of fear. Come out, or I'll climb in after you!"

NEWCOMEN FOUND the door, but his fingers recognized the strength of thick oak crosspieces. The iron plate of the lock was as big as two hands.

He snapped on his cigarette lighter and looked around him. Sacked onions and potatoes filled the air with a sour pungency. From the beams, corn hung on cobs, drying, the color of true gold. It was a storeroom. Two of the windows of it were secured by shutters and wooden pieces nailed across inside. Only the one window was open, the shutters wide, and the crosspieces lying on the floor. He picked up one of them. Part of the nails were rusted black. The other part shone silver bright. They recently had been drawn from the old sockets.

He hesitated, looking toward the window where the white face of Nancy Ormonde appeared.

After a moment, he went out to her.

They hurried down the length of the alley, and came out into the moonlit calm of the great piazza a moment later.

"Did anyone know you were going down that alley, Nancy?" he asked.

They had reached a sidewalk café, and she sank into one of the iron chairs.

"I don't know. The whole world has gone crazy!" she gasped.

"Think back. What's the last time that you mentioned the alleys?" demanded Newcomen.

"I'm trying to think. I haven't talked about them at all, not for a week."

"Where was that?"

"At the Jimmy Mortimer house."

"Who was there?"

"Everybody. It was a huge party."

"But whom did you talk to particularly?"

"I don't remember, Tony. I'm trying to think—I talked to twenty people."

"All the four Mortimers were there?"

"Yes."

"Lucardo?"

"Yes, the *marchese* was there. But that poor, fat-faced—"

"Never mind. I'm not accusing Lucardo. Who else?"

"Dinah Moore, I remember."

"Ah, Dinah was there?"

"With Tom Decker."

"Bertelli? Nicholas Decker? They're both friends of Jimmy Mortimer."

"Yes, they both were there."

"Nicholas Decker, Lucardo, Bertelli, Dinah Moore. Anybody else I know?"

"Only poor, dried-up Hugh Churchill, the secretary. Tony, it

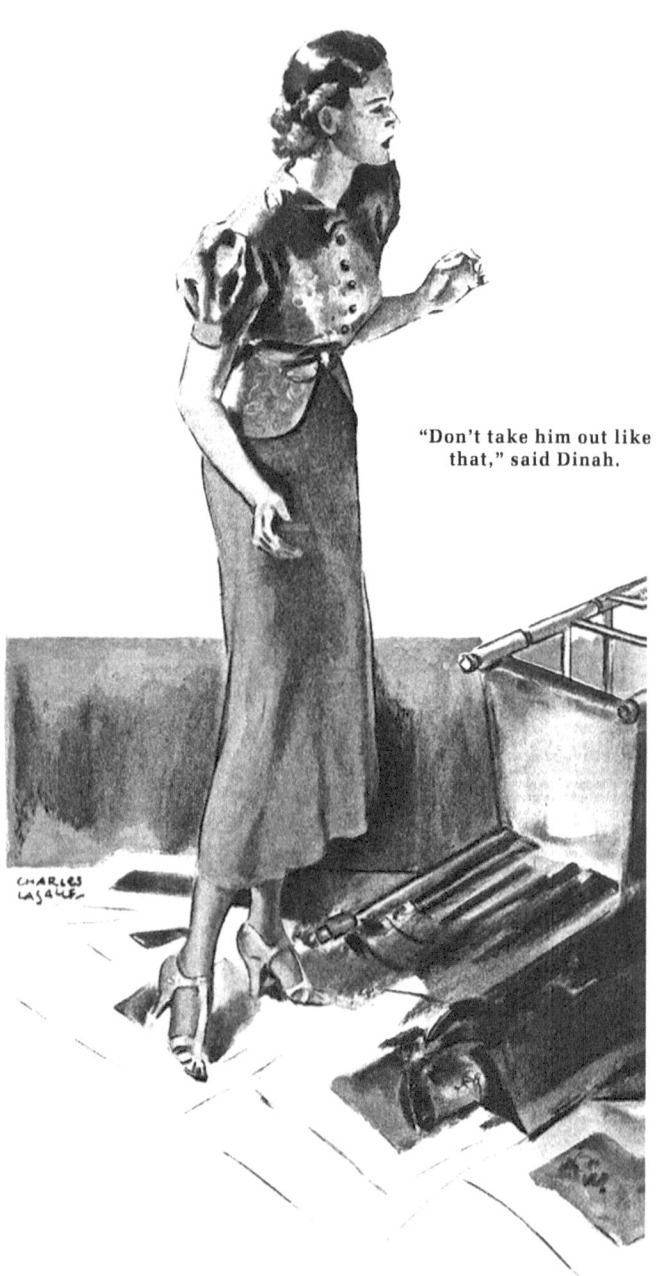

"Don't take him out like that," said Dinah.

was *murder,* your *murder,* that was attempted back there!"

"It was a miss," said Newcomen.

"There's a gendarme. Tell him…"

She sprang up.

"Let the thing go," said Newcomen. "The man— or lady—in that window back there, was taking a pot shot at you, not at me, Nancy."

"I never heard of anything so crazy, Tony!"

"No? You talk a week ago about the alleys. You say that you're going to see them again the first night you have a chance. The most romantic place in the world. Wasn't that it?"

"I suppose I may have said that."

"Well, someone heard you. That's all. And laid the trap. Not a difficult thing to do. Simply to prepare that old store-room and wait every evening. Just requires

"I'll restore him before I show him the door," said Newcomen.

patience... But who could hate you as patiently as all that, Nancy?"

"I don't know! Tony, I want to go home!"

ON THE morning of the fourth day since the murder of Thomas Decker, Marchese Lucardo drove his old car through the gate of the Villa Oliviera. When he reached the house, Hugh Churchill was waiting for him in the dimness of the great hall.

"We'll go straight up to my rooms," said Churchill.

But Lucardo in his leisurely way paused and examined the bottom of a picture frame which hung near the foot of the stairs.

"What is this old gash in the wood?" he asked. "I've seen it before and asked Thomas Decker, but he always forgot to answer."

"Well," said Churchill, pausing, "at last he had to answer everything—everything."

He said the last through his teeth. Then he pointed across the hall.

"You see those old weapons yonder?" he asked. "That group of them decorating the corner? The short-handled battle-axe is the one that sank into that picture frame. And Mr. Decker wouldn't talk about it. Naturally he wouldn't."

"Did *he* do it?" murmured Lucardo, lifting his simple face and looking at the secretary.

"Not he," said Churchill, then: "You said on the telephone that you wanted to see me?"

"I thought it would be well to bring you a small payment, Mr. Churchill, as an evidence of good faith," said Lucardo. "So I brought over a thousand lire. Please take it."

He put the bills in the hand of the secretary, and Churchill made a gesture as though he would throw the money back.

"A thousand lire? Chicken feed!" he said. "We were talking about fifty thousand. *Signor* Marchese!"

"This is merely an earnest of what is to come," said Lucardo. "I am communicating with a banker in London. I have hopes of raising a considerable sum there. But to get money here in Florence..."

"Why not?" demanded Churchill. "You have enough stuff in your house to stock a museum. Pictures, furniture, statues, everything. You could sell some of that and never miss it!"

"Ah, perhaps," said Lucardo, "but there is no market now for such things. If I were forced to sell. I would not realize a quarter of the real value."

"In this world," said Churchill, "I discover that business is business and nothing else. Mr. Decker never hesitated to grind me—he never troubled about my feelings. Marchese Lucardo, I have testimony that will throw you into the hands of the police. Unless I have fifty thousand lire, at once... In a pinch, *Signor* Marchese, there is always that picture by Pontormo, the two saints by the well. I would take that in place of the money."

"Take that?" cried the *marchese,* staring. "It is the treasure of the collection! I would rather give blood than that."

"I'd rather have money than blood," said Churchill. "But whatever I get, I must have it at once."

"At once?" groaned Lucardo. "How much time do you give me?"

"Forty-eight hours!" said the secretary sternly.

"What? Two days? But there would not even be time to advertise a sale!" pleaded Lucardo.

"You can put up the furnishings of your villa as a pledge, however," said Churchill, "and then get the money from a bank."

"Three days, for heaven's sake!" cried the *marchese.*

"Three days? Well, I'm a good-natured fellow," said Churchill. "Three days let it be."

ALDO BERTELLI, even while Lucardo was talking with Hugh Churchill, sat with Dinah Moore in that big room whose French windows gave on the silver tops of the olive trees outside.

"I was talking with Nancy Ormonde about you the other day," he had said when he called, "and she says that you have some charming drawings. I'm not a connoisseur, but I'd like to see them, if I may."

That was why she brought him to the upper room and he watched her unlock the old safe which stood in a comer of the chamber. It was of a type which any professional yegg would have smiled at. Five minutes and a "can-opener" would have forced its door, but it was a reasonable security against ordinary thieves. She unlocked it now and took out a stack of her drawings.

"You'll smile when you see them," she said. "But a little while ago I began to think they might have a value; and if they have, I'm afraid to let them lie about."

"I'd love to see them," said Bertelli, holding out his hand for the stack.

"Sit down there by the window," said the girl. "Here—this chair has a good light. Then I can give them to you one by one."

"You mustn't trouble," said Bertelli, with a certain urgency. "I cannot keep you standing. Let me have them. They will all have an interest for me."

"Will they?" she answered, looking closely at him.

"Of course they will," said the big voice of Newcomen from the door.

Bertelli started around.

"Excuse me for walking in," said Newcomen to the girl. "I found the front door open and just wandered in and kept on wandering. You were up here the other night looking for something, weren't you, Bertelli?"

"Up here? At night?" said Bertelli, beginning to frown, Newcomen squinted at him with care.

"I don't think I'm wrong," he said. "It was only the impression of a moment, by night, with no more light than the flash of a gun gives. But I think you were here the other night, Bertelli. Why?"

"*Signori,*" said Bertelli, "there is something in your tone that I do not choose to understand."

"Dinah, I'm occupied with *Signor* Bertelli," said Newcomen.

The girl walked to the tall windows and out onto the balcony.

Newcomen said: "You've shown me a deal of attention once or twice, recently, Bertelli. I can stand that better than your attentions to Dinah Moore. I think the door is still open, downstairs."

Bertelli drew himself up and bowed.

"It is more than enough," he said. "You need not trouble yourself any further. It is a sufficient insult, *Signor* Newcomen. A friend of mine will wait on you and—"

"Ah, you're talking about a duel, are you?" said Newcomen. "Then I'll give you the best reason of all."

Bertelli saw the danger while it was still in the air but he could not dodge the fist. It struck him half on the neck, half on the root of the jaw, and he slithered down the wall to the floor in a loose heap.

Newcomen picked him up by the scruff of the neck.

"Don't take him out like that," said Dinah Moore, in the calmest of voices, "a little cold water in his face will—"

"I'll restore him before I show him the door," said Newcomen.

He walked out the door with Bertelli dragging his length behind, and so down the stairs, the feet of the Italian thumping loudly from step to step. By the time they were passing through the living room, Bertelli began to recover his wits and struggle to regain his feet. Newcomen permitted that only when he was outside the front door. He stood back, then, and watched Bertelli stagger and weave until his legs were steady. The whole side of his face was blotched with red.

"You look all right," said Newcomen. "People won't notice anything. But how's the proud Italian heart, Bertelli? Burning up, isn't it?"

"*Dio—santo!*" whispered Bertelli with pale lips.

"If you want more trouble out of it," said Newcomen, "you can have it. I hear you're a duellist, Bertelli. Well, there's enough Italy in me to make me handy with a small sword myself. Get out of my sight before I smack you down again. And if I find you sneaking around the *villino* again, I'll twist your neck till it breaks."

HE TURNED his back on Bertelli and went back into the house. Dinah Moore was entering the room from the foot of the stairs. Her composure was perfectly undisturbed.

"Was he the one who shot at you the other night?" she asked.

"I think so," said Newcomen. "He's behind us now, so don't bother about him. But why was he here? What did he want?"

Dinah shook her head, puzzled. "Nancy Ormonde said my drawings might be worth money. But I hardly think so. Just a heap of old and new work of mine. If he wanted something, he merely used the drawings as an excuse."

"Where do you keep them?"

"In the safe."

"Mind if I look?"

"Not at all."

Dinah Moore had replaced the drawings in the safe. She took them out and set them aside. There was nothing else in the safe but a few old papers, inconsequential receipts and the like. Newcomen examined them carefully, but found nothing that could conceivably interest Bertelli.

"He was here for something," grunted Newcomen. Dinah put back the drawings. They returned to the other room.

"I want to make a business proposition to you, Anthony," said the girl slowly. She held out a fold of money. "I want you to take it back and let me go."

"Is that the twenty-five hundred advance payment I gave you?"

She nodded.

"What's happened to you?" asked Newcomen. "You wanted that money for somebody, didn't you?"

"Yes."

"A man, eh?"

"Yes."

"Well, he still needs it, doesn't he? Men who take money from girls never stop needing help."

She said nothing.

"You only have to stick it out for three more days and you clean up five thousand. What makes you want to cut and run?"

"Anthony, reasons won't matter with you. But will you let me go?"

"How badly do you want to go?"

"It's more than wanting. I *have* to go."

"Why?"

"I can't tell you."

"Come, come!" said Newcomen. "Let's not be mysterious."

She drew a great breath, staring at him.

"No," she murmured to herself. "No, you won't let me go. You're going to keep me to the end."

"To the seventh day. I suppose I am," said Newcomen.

"But there's your own danger!" cried the girl.

"What danger?" he asked.

"They tried to murder you last night—and you ask me what danger?"

"You heard about that shot in the alley? It was at Nancy Ormonde. Not at me."

"It was not at her. She jumped in front of you. And then the shooting stopped."

"Stories spread fast in Florence. But you're wrong about it. The murderer lost heart. The sound of his gun frightened him," stated Newcomen. "Somebody Nancy jilted. Somebody like that was trying to get even."

"You know that's not true," she answered.

"It's the way I choose to look at it," he said. "Do we have lunch?"

She looked at him and made a silent surrender. Then she rose and left. Newcomen sat down to look over the darkened room, the sheen of the waxed tiles, the vague images which reflected in that surface, the bigness, the sense of space and air.

They had lunch quietly in a sort of forced calm, *fritto misto*, a bottle of Rhine wine pale with the dew of the icebox. Then Newcomen was called to the telephone.

The moment he heard the voice, he settled himself in a chair, at ease for much talking.

"Of course not," he said. "I slept perfectly. And you?"

"I couldn't sleep a wink," said Nancy Ormonde.

Dinah Moore brought an ash tray and a cigarette. She put the cigarette in his mouth and lighted it. Newcomen nodded at her through the smoke.

"It *was* a shock, of course," said Newcomen.

Dinah Moore was leaving the room. He put his hand over the mouthpiece of the phone and called: "Dinah, come back!"

SHE SAT down with her back to him.

"Tony, can you dream who fired that shot at you?" asked Nancy.

"I can dream. But I'm not sure. Somebody who has a headache at this moment, I think."

"Whom do you mean?"

"It doesn't matter. I don't want to talk about that. I want to talk about a girl who looked death in the face and didn't care."

"I did care, Tony. I was horribly frightened."

"How many men have seen a girl risk her life for him; not because she loved him, either."

"I'm not so sure. Tony."

"Aren't you? That's not just kindness, I hope. But that bit you did, threw a light on you. A halo, Nancy, to my eyes."

"You're not going to make an angel of me, Tony?"

"All except wings that might carry you away," said Newcomen, breathing out a yawn behind his hand. "When can I see you?"

"Any time. Now, for instance."

"I'm sorry. But I can't today."

"You have to spend the time with Dinah Moore. Is that it?"

"About the chapel frescoes."

"Oh, Tony, you dreadful liar!"

"Tomorrow? I'll telephone."

"And don't forget—on account of frescoes and things."

"I won't. Good-bye."

He hung up.

"Is Nancy Ormonde falling in love with you?" asked Dinah Moore.

"Nancy? Oh, Nancy doesn't simply fall, do you think?"

"What would you call it?"

"She merely decides," said Newcomen.

"Do you think that she's as cold-blooded as that?" asked the girl.

"I don't know. What do you think, Dinah?"

"We don't think about one another," she answered.

"Do you *siesta?*" he asked.

"Usually. I don't have to."

"You could lie down on that couch and I on this one," said Newcomen.

"I'll read," she said. "Do you want to be wakened at any special time?"

"No, this is already a special time," he said.

He stretched himself on a couch, pulled a pillow under his head, and took from his pocket a small green tassel. He began to pass the silk threads slowly through his fingertips, as though absent-minded, his head turned to watch her.

Dinah went to the bookshelves in the corner of the room.

"Do lie down and rest," said Newcomen.

"Well…" she said, turning slowly, yawning a little.

"Take off that hot dress and slip on something cool and light," he suggested.

"What color shall it be?" she asked.

"I've seen you in a charming dressing gown," said Newcomen.

"Have you?"

"The green one," said Newcomen. "It was this color."

He held up the silk tassel, and, watching closely—he had to watch very closely indeed to see—he observed the quick little tremor that ran through her. She went to him and took the tassel from his fingers.

"Where did you find it, Anthony?" she asked.

"Why, you'd never guess, would you?" said Newcomen.

"I don't know," she answered. "Where did you find it?"

"I found it in Tom Decker's studio."

"The studio..." breathed the girl.

"On the floor," he said, "close to the telephone table."

She moved back, as though she wanted a better chance to look at his face, with distance for clear perspective.

"When?" she asked.

"Why, I found it there the morning Decker died," said Newcomen.

She sank slowly onto the couch opposite him.

"The morning he died..." she echoed.

"And I've had it in my pocket ever since, as a matter of fact."

"That same morning, you saw *me* in a green dressing gown," she stated. "And you noticed that a tassel was gone from the belt of the dressing gown, didn't you?" she asked.

"Did I?" said Newcomen, absently.

A long silence followed.

"You will *siesta*, won't you, Dinah?" he asked.

She stood up.

"I'll—yes," she said.

"You'll come back soon?" he asked.

"Yes," she answered.

"Do come soon," said Newcomen, and listened to the soft closing of the door.

THE PILLOW raised Newcomen's head to such a height that he was able to look into the tall mirror that hung on the opposite wall, and in it he could observe the greater part of the wall behind his head, including the door through which Dinah Moore had just gone. Over it was placed a Madonna between two adoring angels in blue and white Della Robbia ware. This was not fitted into a wall niche but merely hung on brackets, and there was a certain amount of play in the setting so that the vibration caused by the door sent a slight tremor through the plaque. The mirror exaggerated the motion.

To the left of the door hung a Venetian landscape with sheep and trees and blue running water, and a pair of absurd eighteenth-century lovers in their best and silliest clothes. To the right of the door stood a tall chest of drawers, a very good and old piece. All of this lay within the field embraced by the mirror's reflection. Newcomen, almost closing his eyes, studied the Madonna and the angels through his lashes and seemed asleep.

He was incommoded by the size of the automatic under his coat and turned a little to give it more room. After that, he lay motionless, watching the mirror.

Something like five or ten minutes went by slowly before he saw the bright Della Robbia piece tremble again; and then the door opened. There was no sound. It pushed open perhaps a foot, and Newcomen strained his eyes to get a glimpse of the figure in the hall behind it, but it was like staring at something in a twilight mist.

He could discover the outlines, but not the face. He could not even be sure whether it were man or woman. It was all as vague as an indistinct recollection out of infancy, one of those memories which are more illusion and fancy than hard fact.

The door at last closed again, soundlessly. It seemed to Newcomen that a ghost had entered the room.

Newcomen took a deeper breath.

And two or three minutes still passed before the girl returned to the room in the green dressing gown.

"That's good," said Newcomen, in a sleepy voice. "It's a nice, cool color."

"The belt has two tassels now," said Dinah Moore. "I suppose you're glad of that?"

"It *is* a relief," said Newcomen.

He smiled at her, but she did not smile in return. She went over to the opposite couch and lay down on it.

"Are you going to sleep?" she asked.

"Absolutely," he said.

She was silent again. Newcomen stretched himself, turned his head toward the back of the couch, and almost at once his regular breathing became more audible, slower, more deep in vibration. The girl, listening, smiled a little.

"It's a good pretense," she said softly, "but you did it a little too quickly. People wouldn't fall asleep as quickly as that in real life, would they?"

He did not answer. He did not stir.

And she, after a moment, turned her head suddenly, and stared across the room. She saw the hand of Newcomen slide from his breast to the couch beside him and remain there, the fingers loose.

SHE STOOD up, frowning, and crossed the room to him, stepping slowly and carefully. Even when she stood just above him, she was not certain. She bent and peered more closely at his face, noting above all a certain loosening of the lines about the mouth, a slight swelling of the lips. The lines in the forehead were less sharply cut also.

She continued to stand there for a few moments, until the thing was entirely clear in her mind. Newcomen actually was asleep or else he was a matchless actor.

She returned to her own couch. She did not sleep for a considerable interval. The thoughts which passed in her mind caused her eyes to widen, brighten, and only gradually they grew dim again. She was certain that sleep would not by any means overcome her; and then she was aware of someone sitting beside her, and knew, by the deep gulf of weariness through which she was rousing, that she had been in profound slumber for a long time.

She blinked her eyes to make sure, and saw that Newcomen was reading a book in a chair which he had drawn up close to the couch, only leaving space between the leg of his chair and the side of the couch for the German dog. He was turning a page now. She watched the care and automatic skill with which the big forefinger slid down the edge, lifted the page, turned it with a continuous and yet slow movement which prevented the slightest crackling sound.

She watched him for some moments. Presently, without looking from the page, he said: "A good sleep, Dinah?"

"Yes, a good sleep," she answered.

"It's a sign of a clear conscience, isn't it," asked Newcomen, "when one wakes up slowly, with wide-open eyes, smiling a little?"

"I wasn't smiling," she said.

"Ah, but you were," said Newcomen.

"You can't tell, Anthony. You didn't even glance at me."

"I didn't need to," said Newcomen. "I was watching you with my mind's eye. I know just how you will look under any circumstances. Asleep or waking... with or without tassels."

"It's terribly late!" she exclaimed, looking out the window. For all the eastern trees were covered by the shadow of the house.

"Just pleasantly late," said Newcomen. "Too late for tea, I suppose, and only a fraction too early for cocktails. By the time you've yawned twice, we can start having cocktails... I'll go to the villa and change and come back."

He was back in the villa and had changed his clothes when the butler came, saying: "*Signor* Bertelli wishes to speak to you. Are you in, *signore?*"

"Connect me," said Newcomen.

BERTELLI SAID over the wire, in a soft but distinct voice: "*Signor* Newcomen, if I do nothing more about what happened today, does it prove that I am a coward?"

"I think not," said Newcomen. "I think it merely proves that you're biding your time."

"Shall we let it go at that, then? In the meantime, we can be of practical use to one another. I have something to sell."

"I'm not a collector," said Newcomen.

"But of information?"

"That may be different. Information about what?"

"About your dead friend, Thomas Decker."

"What about him, *Signor* Bertelli?"

"I wish to tell you the name of his murderer," said Bertelli.

"Ah, that would be worth knowing," said Newcomen, "if it's not that fellow Emilio in the prison."

"You know that it's not he," said Bertelli.

"Not at all," answered Newcomen.

"You know perfectly well," said Bertelli, in the same low, clear voice, the words carefully clipped off, "that the butler had nothing to do with the murder. That is why you are conducting your own investigation."

"Ah, am I investigating?"

"So busily," said Bertelli, "that there are people who feel that you are trying to cover up your own traces."

"In Florence," said Newcomen, "there are always a few people who are capable of thinking anything."

Bertelli allowed a silence to intervene for an instant.

"Concerning my proposal," he said at last, and something in that quiet voice suggested to Newcomen a mind strained to the uttermost by a nervous tension.

"It would be worth something to me, of course," said Newcomen.

"How much?" asked Bertelli.

"Why, ten thousand lire, say?"

"A hundred thousand lire, perhaps?" asked Bertelli.

"Too much!" said Newcomen.

"A hundred and fifty thousand lire, say?" said Bertelli.

"My dear fellow," laughed Newcomen. "You're not serious, of course. That's quite a fortune. A hundred and fifty thousand?"

He laughed again.

The voice of Bertelli cut short his laughter, as the Italian said: "Suppose we say two hundred thousand lire?"

There was a pause.

Newcomen said, sharply: "I'll take that offer."

"The price rose while you waited," said Bertelli calmly. "It is now a quarter of a million lire."

"I accept!" said Newcomen. "Will you come up here now?"

"I can't come there now," said Bertelli.

"Why not?"

"The doctor confines me to my bed."

"Sick?"

"Indisposed. When I see you, no one must know about it."

"I'll see you wherever you say. Bologna, perhaps?"

"Instead of going a distance, let us meet in a crowd."

"Perfect! I'll give a party tomorrow."

"One already is being given. The Marchese Lucardo. Will you be there?"

"If I'm asked."

"I'll see that you are. At six-thirty, say?"

"You want an advance payment?"

"*Signore,* I must trust everything to your honor."

"My honor? Very well!" said Newcomen. "This doctor—he's taking good care of you, Bertelli?"

"He is a clever man. Good-bye, *Signor* Newcomen."

"One moment. You'll take care of yourself?"

"I shall."

"Who is this doctor?"

"Doctor Ferrando."

"I know him. At six-thirty tomorrow, at Lucardo's. Good-bye!"

THE MANNERS of all Italians above a certain class are perfect and only degenerate under the influence of a bad marriage, that is to say, an unprofitable one. As a rule, the educated man is only a boor when it pays to be one. Doctor Ferrando was fitted with manners as sleek as a thin kid glove, and even over the telephone he conveyed a special unction. He smiled continually and bowed a little to the receiver as he talked.

"I'm out of sorts," said big Newcomen over the wire. "Can you run up to see me right away? I have an evening engagement."

"Tomorrow, perhaps?" said Doctor Ferrando.

"This evening. Now, please," urged Newcomen. "A special favor to me, Doctor Ferrando."

"My dear *Signor* Newcomen, I cancel everything else at once and come to you as fast as the automobile will take me," said the doctor.

And all the way to the Villa Oliviera he doubled the usual fee and then undoubled it. He was in a pleasant misery. The rich should pay more, and the rich Americans should pay still more. But unfortunately the old golden days when well-to-do Americans paid today and reckoned tomorrow seem to have departed forever. They seem to expect to pay not more than twice what others would be charged. Doctor Ferrando was in a perspiration before he got out at the big villa. He had not been able to make up his mind.

The first look at Newcomen made him add fifty lire to the bill on the strength of youth; but with the second look he subtracted the extra fifty. He could not tell what to think.

Newcomen said: "The fact is that I'm not up to snuff. A bit groggy in the mornings, and a bit lethargic through the day. I wonder if the old blood pressure is right or if the liver is out of whack, or something like that."

Ferrando made an examination. He punched at the liver and located it obscurely behind a sheathing of abdominal muscle strong enough to gird up the loins of a horse. He listened with his stethoscope to a heart-beat as loud and steady as the tramping of the same horse over an iron bridge.

Ferrando stepped back and polished his spectacles, and then brushed his mustaches with the tips of his fingers. The glasses added profundity to his judgments, the mustaches doubled the smartness of his air.

"As a matter of fact," said the doctor, "it is not difficult to see that there is a touch of liverish condition. That would account for the symptoms you complain of. You drink cocktails, *Signor* Newcomen?"

"I do."

"Avoid them," suggested Ferrando. "Also, oranges and eggs are bad for the liver. It will make only a slight variation in your diet, but an essential one. And then if you get to bed a little earlier at night, you will feel a new man, *signore*."

"I'll do exactly as you say," said Newcomen, as he pulled on his clothes. "My friend Bertelli says that you are the best man in Italy."

"Ah, you know *Signor* Bertelli?"

"Intimately."

"A very charming man," said Ferrando.

"A pity that he should be upset just now," said Newcomen.

"Well, we are no longer children."

"Exactly," said Newcomen. "What would you say about Aldo? Nothing seriously wrong?"

"Nerves—what is there to say about nerves?" asked Ferrando.

"Without them man would be a beast, eh? With them he suffers like a poor devil. A pity. *Signor* Newcomen."

"Mr. Thomas Decker…" said Newcomen.

"Ah, a terrible misfortune," said Ferrando.

"Mr. Decker…"

"To me, a personal loss. Permit me to beg you to believe me. A personal loss," said the doctor. "Such a waste—and at the hands of a butler."

"Ridiculous," said Newcomen.

"Absurd," said Ferrando.

"Poor Tom Decker was troubled with bad nerves from time to time," observed Newcomen.

"Very often," agreed Ferrando. "Often I had him in my care for that very weakness. A battery overcharged is soon worn out. May I use that comparison?"

"A man with an eye like yours," said Newcomen, "sees twice as much as the ordinary fellow like me."

"In my profession, the eyes must be used, of course."

"Naturally," said Newcomen. "If he had been more nervous than usual just before the end, you would have noticed it, doctor, of course."

"Of course," said Ferrando. "And in fact he *was* more nervous than usual. I gave him, that same day, a double sedative. Not an opiate but a hypnotic."

"Tom Decker had grown to hate the night time, hadn't he?" asked Newcomen.

"The very thing," said the doctor. "One grows used to trouble by day, but its face becomes hideous at night. It is the unknown that we fear."

"Of course," agreed Newcomen. "And Tom Decker had become afraid of the night?"

"He hated to see the setting of the sun. Just before the end, he was in a bad state."

"Did the bad state come on him suddenly?"

"Quite."

"That very day perhaps?"

"Yes. Exactly. That very day he suddenly was extremely nervous."

"This Florentine air is very soothing," suggested Newcomen, "but sometimes it plays tricks on us, perhaps? And the nerves go crash like Tom Decker's?"

"Exactly so," said the doctor.

"Or Bertelli's, for instance?"

"In the same class, entirely."

"As though a man suddenly became afraid?"

"Exactly as though he became afraid."

"A sort of dread of the night and the unknown, you say?"

"There is no better way of putting it."

"Thank you for coming. I'll follow your orders. Good-bye, Doctor Ferrando."

"It is a pleasure to serve you," said Ferrando, and left with a light step, for he was sure that he had not come to that house for the last time. Some people are limited in the number of illnesses they can afford to have, but money is a blessing to the idle rich and to the doctors who take care of them.

NEWCOMEN WENT down through the twilight to the *villino* where Dinah Moore lived. He took the long way around because he did not feel like climbing stone walls in his dinner jacket and patent leather shoes.

He found the table set for two on the terrace outside the house. There was only the light of two candles under glass hoods, besides the dimness of the moon which was just pushing up through the eastern trees. Dinah Moore moved toward him from the shadows.

"An old-fashioned scene," said Newcomen. "A girl, a moon and a garden."

"With a modern touch," she said, smiling gravely.

"What's the modern touch?"

"Young man in dinner jacket and gun."

"Am I carrying a gun?" said Newcomen.

"Your clothes fit beautifully, of course. They always do. The gun disturbs the line just a trifle."

"Do you think I am being melodramatic—carrying a gun when I am invited to dinner with a girl in a garden under the moon?"

Dinah shook her head. They moved toward the table. "If you feel you are in danger, of course. Take that chair, so that you can watch the moon. Dinner will be here presently."

"You don't feel any sense of danger, Dinah?"

She looked at him across the table. "Yes," she answered frankly. "Ever since Tom Decker died."

"Since Tom Decker was murdered," he corrected.

"But not the sort of danger that can be warded off with a gun."

"And yet you have a defense?"

He rose a little from his chair before she could answer.

"What is it?" she asked in a low voice.

"Have you thought of everything for this evening?" he answered in a voice equally low.

"I hope so," she replied.

"I think you have," murmured Newcomen. "I think that you've even thought of hiring an audience for us."

He sprang from the table suddenly with the naked automatic in his hand.

"Come out in the open!" he called in Italian, facing a patch of big shrubs.

A crackling of footfalls through the brush, a sound as of a rushing wind answered him; and Newcomen plunged in pursuit.

HE WENT through the brush like a stone through a glass. Beyond, turning the corner of a potted lemon tree, he had a glimpse of the fugitive. The moon brushed a hand of silver over the face of Roberto, the former cook. Then he was lost as he dodged behind the tree.

He ran fast, but not like a sprinter of Newcomen's quality. Newcomen called: "I'll fire, Roberto. Stand where you are!"

Then he ran out from behind the potted lemons and had a glimpse of the coattails of Roberto as the cook vanished into the shadows under a little grove of cypresses. Newcomen, the moment he was among them, halted and stood still. The noise of running feet no longer pounded the earth. Before him, the narrow tree trunks ruled black lines across the moonshine. Merely to turn the head dazzled the eyes with jet black and brilliant white.

Roberto could not be far off. Perhaps he had given up the flight and was preparing himself, behind one of the trunks, to strike back at his pursuer; or perhaps he was stealing away.

Newcomen added up the chances, made his choice, and ran on again, breaking quickly out of the tree shadows into the comparative open of scattering olive trees, bent and twisted by time.

The way a rabbit gets up from behind a tuft of grass, a man's silhouette sprang away from the crooked trunk of an olive tree. Roberto was there, running frantically, swaying a bit from side to side with effort, his head pitching back with every stride, like a miler finishing his exhausting race. But Newcomen ran easily up on him. He was reaching a hand for the Italian as Roberto came near the boundary wall. Roberto screamed as he dodged, and leaped straight up at the top of the barrier. He struck it, sprawling over, and toppled down on the farther side.

Newcomen heard the body strike with a solid force as he swung himself up to the top of the wall. He dropped down beside Roberto, who lay with his head twisted under one shoulder, motionless. When Newcomen turned the body, he heard the grating of broken bones in the neck.

He pressed his ear to the breast of the Italian. There was no tremor of the heart. He was dead. And at the same time the whine of a motor climbed the hill.

Newcomen swung back over the wall. The automobile wavered its headlight over the brow of the hill. Above the edge of the wall Newcomen saw the car stop. Two men climbed out, bent over Roberto, and then loaded the inert body into their machine. They drove on, and Newcomen faced the *villino* again.

He went slowly back to the dinner table. The candles made a vaguely flickering light, a running of faint shadows, across the moonlit tablecloth. That was the only sign of life. The maid was not there. The girl had left her chair.

He lifted his head to listen, and in the effort to clear his senses, he almost closed his eyes; but there was no sound nearer than the main road toward Florence. No wind blew. The shadows lay still beneath the cypresses. From the kitchen of the *villino* he heard not the least sound of rattling dishes.

He had left a living scene and returned to one as dead as paint. But by degrees he felt life re-enter the surroundings, a faint sense of it, as single as one ray of light in darkness, and as dangerous as the blade of a sharp knife. Then he opened his eyes. The danger did not lie around him on the ground. He felt it, coldly, raining an influence from above; and when he looked up, he saw in the black arch of the tower casement, Dinah Moore, with the moon white upon her face.

"Dinah!" he called, and found himself looking at the empty darkness of the window from which she had disappeared.

Newcomen ran for the house. There was a cold horror in his blood and he tried to drive it out by the speed with which he climbed the stairs, still remembering the white of the face that had looked down on him and the inhuman, stone-cut smile.

He had to pass down the upper hall to reach the stairs that led into the tower. They went round and round in a spiral that was cut through the unnecessary thick of the wall. He passed one small chamber with the checked pattern of the window bars cast by the moonlight across the floor. He reached the highest story of the tower, and stood for a moment in the dark at the head of the stairs.

Down in the hollow among the villagers someone was playing an accordion, a crazy jazz-time tune as out of place to Newcomen as the tunes of a music box in a room of death. The moonlight poured through the open arch at which he had seen the girl. The curve of the arch lay brilliantly cut into the black upon the floor. He saw nothing else, but he remained there for a moment.

After that, he crossed to the empty window space where the girl had stood. From this point he could see the small table below, the moon-white on the tablecloth strangely qualified even at this distance by the yellow glow of the candle flames. He could tell the difference in color between the wine in the narrow glasses and the water in the big ones. Only the silver melted strangely into the brightness of the moonshine.

That uneasiness which he had felt when he first stood by the table had returned to him. He swung sharply about and stared into the shadows which poured the corners of the tower-room full.

He gritted his teeth as he tried to make out the puzzle. She could not have run down the stairs as fast as he had come up them, and yet she was gone.

He moved toward the other side of the floor and stumbled over a heap of shadow and softness. The shock of it stopped him an instant with electricity shooting out through his fingertips and up into the roots of his hair; then he lifted the body.

The head of Dinah Moore fell back over his arm with the white of the moonshine turning her face to stone.

NEWCOMEN BENT to press his ear against Dinah's breast with a terrible intuition that it would be with her as with Roberto in the open highway; and then he heard the faint murmur of the heart like a watch under a pillow.

He carried her down the winding of the stairs to her big room and laid her on the couch there. He wet a towel in the bathroom and put the cold of it to her throat.

She made no sound. She did not stir. It was only after a long moment that he saw her eyes were open, watching his movements intently. Something in her silence at that moment seemed to him utterly inhuman. He tried her pulse. It was already strong and very fast.

She was better. There was no use asking questions about how she felt.

"What was it, Dinah?" he asked. "What happened to you, up there?"

She closed her eyes and shook her head a little. Her eyes remained closed.

"Did he die, Anthony?" she whispered.

"He's dead," said Newcomen.

"Did he talk before he died?"

"Not a word."

She opened her eyes and looked straight up toward the ceiling. It seemed to Newcomen that her next breath was deeper, as though in relief.

He stepped hack to reach a chair, but her hand moved out toward him.

"Will you stay with me?" she asked.

"I'll stay," said Newcomen.

She closed her eyes again.

He sat down after he had pulled up a deep chair close to her. The time went by him with a soft whisper. Now and then he turned his head toward the window behind him, or the French windows that opened on the balcony above the loggia, on the right. But as a rule he watched nothing except the girl, studying her as though he were reading a page of difficult print, such as one of those big, time-faded pages of an early folio, so kind to the touch and so bathing to the eyes. By her breathing, she was now asleep.

He remained perhaps for ten minutes in this posture before he heard a breathing in the room. There had been no footfall, but now he was certain that he heard breathing, incredibly fast. He turned his head slowly, his jaw set hard, toward the door. Nothing appeared in it at the height of a man, but a figure seemed to be crouching there not much higher than the knees of a tall man.

The sound of the breathing unquestionably came from it. Then Hans moved stealthily out into the very faint light of the room. The big dog with his soundless feet paused in front of Newcomen to show him the white of his fangs and the green of his eyes. He went on and looked at his mistress, then lay down on the floor beside the couch. He was hot and tired from a run, apparently, but he did not slump down. He lowered himself like a hunting beast that knows when noise is not advisable.

ONE WHO stays in a room long enough, quietly enough, finds that time adds a fourth dimension to everything around him, just as the hunter in the hide at last sees the forest come to life. So for Newcomen, the room at last had a moving, breathing vitality. He lay inert in the chair with his eyes almost closed, and the inaction of his body left his mind more alert. If he stared at the girl, it seemed to him that the shadows behind him began to slide quietly across the floor toward his back. And if he glanced away from Dinah Moore, he always could see her opening her eyes behind his back and sitting up stealthily, with an ominous face.

When, at last, there was a movement, it was Hans who stood up from the floor. His panting had stopped long since and now he stepped utterly without sound, coming to Newcomen and looking at him with fixed eyes for a long moment. Afterward the dog turned his head toward Dinah Moore and went so close to her that she must have felt his breath.

He carried her down
the winding of the
stairs... she made no
sound... did not stir.

These studies of Hans were, it appeared, to make sure that both his mistress and Newcomen were asleep. When he had satisfied himself, he moved across the room. Newcomen watched the crooked course through which the dog selected only places covered with the rugs and never stepped on the bare tiles where the scratching of his claws might make the slightest noise. He went to the open French windows and disappeared.

Newcomen turned from Dinah and went softly across the room to the balcony beyond the French windows.

The shadows cast by the moon had now shrunk close to the feet of the trees; the olives were clouds of silver-grey. All things seemed to be clearly revealed, and yet every shadow was deep enough to defy the eye, and all edges, all outlines, lacked sharp detail.

Something rustled through the grass, a sound like that of a passing wind, except that it was more localized. Then Hans came out of the brush into the open, carrying something in his mouth. He looked behind him. He looked to either side. But he did not look up, where Newcomen was watching from the balcony. Instead, he glided off among the shadows, and as soon as he was gone, Newcomen slipped over the balustrade and down a pillar to the ground.

He followed the direction the dog had taken, moving swiftly, and came through the trees in time to see the wolf-dog scale the road wall and disappear on the farther side. The imagination of Newcomen tricked him with the image of Roberto, the cook and poisoner, scrambling over that wall at exactly the same point!

He ran on until he could look over the barrier. At the same moment, Hans leaped up on the far side of the road and vanished over the garden wall of the Villa Oliviera.

Newcomen followed, sweating with haste, down the wall, across the road, and up the farther side until he dropped to the moist ground of the terrace beyond. He was in time to see Hans trotting up to the next level, and Newcomen broke into a skulking run, putting down his feet as carefully as possible, the outer edge of the sole first. Up to the Hercules Terrace he followed behind Hans, and there saw the dog slipping down past the moon-brightened face of the water-lily pond. The dark mouth of the grotto opened just beyond. Here Hans paused for a moment to look back over his shoulder. Then he entered the blackness.

SO FAR as Newcomen was aware, no rear opening afforded a retreat from the grotto. He kept himself under the black shadow of the trees at the edge of the lawn, and in this shelter approached the mouth of the artificial cave. Close by, he halted. He could hear what he took to be a faint sound of scratching. Then silence. And after a few minutes, Hans appeared again and trotted panting down the length of the terrace, disappearing to the left down the steps which led to the terrace immediately beneath.

Newcomen went to the mouth of the grotto. He leaned and listened. When he heard not a sound from the inside, he made a pace into that thick darkness. The black of it closed over his lips and stifled him like water. He ignited his cigarette lighter. The glow from it danced up and down. The shadows wavering behind the out jutting of the rocks gave a sinister life to the little cave. The solid walls of it seemed in motion.

The cave had a sort of inner ear, a secondary excavation the floor of which was not rock but soft earth, and the sign of the dog's scratching was still on the surface of it. With the toe of his shoe he kicked into the loose of the soil; a fresh mutton bone, clotted with black earth, tumbled out into view.

Newcomen put a hand against the wall of the cave and smiled. He was understanding more things than one. This was the treasure trove of Hans; this was the burial ground which he would excavate in a time of winter famine, if hunger ever overtook him!

Into the freshly disturbed soil, Newcomen rooted again with his foot. Something much lighter than the bone came out, and flashed at him. He leaned above it; staring. At last he picked up a little stiletto which could not have been long in the damp of the ground, for it was only beginning to tarnish, the rust commencing to form in a series of little black spots.

It was a delicate weapon with a hilt so small that obviously one was meant to hold it between the two first fingers, with the thumb pressed down over the butt like a hypodermic. Gripped in that fashion, its blade would penetrate like a needle, deeply without effort. Before the first wasp-sting of pain flashed across the nerves the point would already be entering the heart. Ladies of a more potent and earlier age sometimes armed themselves with these little tools, as with a special grace. The whole hilt and blade, together, were not over five or six inches long.

The lighter began to grow hot in the hand of Newcomen. He snapped down the cover and left the grotto.

At the end of the water-lily pond he paused at the spot where the body of Thomas Decker had fallen.

No doubt, when Hans decided to add this bit to his store it was enriched by the blood of Tom Decker. Newcomen braced back his shoulders and took a deeper breath.

THE MARCHESE LUCARDO was of a nature so simple that it was easy for him to spend a day in any of twenty pursuits. He could walk endlessly down the rows of his orchards and vineyards, talking with the farmers here and there; he might drive up through the mountains and spend many hours half waking, half drowsing over a small *fiasco* of red wine, while his eyes wandered over the view and tasted the differences between highlands and lowlands, with the distances breathed full of mists.

He could be content to spend a day hunting with a shotgun and a dog—or with a camera; or he might fall into talk with the cook and speak not so much about the meals that were to come as about triumphs of the past.

On this afternoon, however, he spent much time talking to the cook and the butler.

He said: "We have many people coming this evening. Let the titbits be very good. Some of those anchovies curled around toothpicks and stuck into those little squares of spiced toast; and the other things, as you have made them before. Let there be enough to leave a wastage afterward. In a big house there always should be a sense of comfort and plenty. For lack of that same plenty, I have caused my son to wander away from me into the expensive world. But all this you know as well as I do. This evening, I wish everything to be perfect. Help me today so that I can help you tomorrow. That is a good proverb."

When he had finished talking in this vein, the marquis went into his office. It was his routine. Considering the familiar weaknesses of his nature, he knew that if he did not submit to some sort of a routine, he never would accomplish anything except to make time flow away too fast, like soundless water down a flume. So he fell to his correspondence.

This morning he had on his desk not only letters but also a small oblong packet with the wrapper addressed in typewriting.

This packet he chose to unravel first of all, and he took from it a little unsigned, typewritten note, which said:

My dear *Marchese:*

Last evening the poisoner, Roberto, who used to be the cook for Dinah Moore, showed his ugly face near her villa again. Either the man is crazy or he is receiving good pay. What do you think?

If he is being paid, how interesting if you could find out the source of his income?

I enclose, by the way, the knife with which Thomas Decker probably was stabbed through the back.

I know that you keep a collection of interesting weapons of all sorts, and perhaps you will enjoy having this about.

Lucardo, when he had finished reading, without looking at the other contents of the packet, smoothed the paper and read again. He lifted the paper to the light and made sure that it had no watermark. He squinted at the lettering, to observe that some of the letters were printed toward the left hand, while others struck a little to the right. The ink was not one even shade, but sometimes darker and sometimes lighter. The letter was written in Italian, but it was plain from the phraseology that an English-speaking person had composed the note. Certain typographical mistakes indicated an amateur at work on the machine.

"An American or an Englishman," ran the thoughts of Lucardo, "who knows something about me and who has very strong hands, to judge by the degree of pressure he used in writing this letter. A cool, steady man, without nerves. It is, of course, *Signor* Newcomen."

When he had reached this conclusion, he picked up the letter, unlocked a steel filing cabinet and put the paper away in a definite place, with great care. Afterward, he made an entry on two separate cards, to make sure of being able to locate the letter again as quickly as possible, whenever he chose.

All of this had been finished before he opened the final wrapping inside the packet and disclosed the little stiletto. Small globules of earth were still attached to it. He observed the spots of rust with interest. He held up the weapon to the light and saw that it still was keen enough to glisten like the end of a dripping icicle.

Afterward, he went into the washroom adjoining his office and washed the stiletto with a good deal of care, seeing that all the liquid ran into a soap dish which, afterward, he emptied into a small flask. The flask he corked, labelled, and gave to a servant with word to take it at once to the commissary of police in Florence. With the flask he sent a brief note:

> Test this to find out if there are traces of human blood. If so, identify the type of blood. Answer at once. Do not wait till tomorrow.
>
> Lucardo.

When he had finished this hit of work, he picked up a book stuck the stiletto into it like a paper knife, and laid the book in plain view upon his desk. The time for his party was approaching when his chauffeur took the flask at full speed into the city.

NEWCOMEN, AT the end of the fifth day since the murder of Thomas Decker, drove Dinah Moore out to the Villa Lucardo to the party. On the way he said to her: "What's the special trouble now, Dinah?"

"You'll find it in the newspapers," she answered. "Roberto was found dead in the road outside the *villino*."

"Ah, was he?"

"Anthony, did you—?"

"He fell from the wall," said Newcomen, shortly.

She turned her head and examined his face.

"Whenever *you* are ready to talk about last night, I'll do my share of chattering," he said.

She did not answer this.

He observed. "The poisoner out of the way—that's good news, isn't it? Or were you fond of Roberto?"

She looked up suddenly, but not at Newcomen. "Fond of him?"she echoed.

"You might have been. Perhaps, that unlucky night, he didn't mean to put the poison on *your* plate. Perhaps he'd forgotten that *you* would be served first. Perhaps he was reasonably sure, Dinah, that the first service would be for your guest? So I was intended. In that case, I would have had a fit and died like the cat. Would you have been sorry about the poor young man after he was gone? Would you, Dinah?"

She drew a breath and then looked away from him.

"Would you have taken his head on your lap, as you did the cat? Would you have soothed his hair as you did the dead cat? With the same thoughtful look?" asked Newcomen.

Here she turned her head and looked steadily at him.

He continued: "Because you have a way of abstracting yourself from even the most exciting moment. If a whole battle began to smash and crash around you, I can imagine Dinah stopping to admire the sound effects, quietly, instead of ducking into the first shell hole. It's admirable, self-control like that; but it seems a little mysterious. And dangerous. Because it's hard to understand. You follow me, Dinah?"

She was still watching him with expressionless eyes.

"You always make yourself clear when you talk with me," she said at last.

He had slowed the car until it merely crawled, the powerful motor taking it on at a walking pace, while the gravel crunched like snow under the tires. The trees went by them slowly, each with a whispering of wind in the branches. Off to the left was the Lucardo Villa, the walls roughed in with greys and yellows.

"Anthony," Dinah said, "why don't you leave Florence? The

next bullet may not miss you. Why don't you turn around and go now?"

"Suppose I take you with me?" asked Newcomen.

"What do you mean?"

"Suppose we went together?"

"Where?" she asked.

"Over the hills and far away," said Newcomen, "Farther away than the end of the seventh day."

HE FELT her glance and turned to her, but only in time to see her eyes close as though she were afraid to open her mind to him.

"You're not smiling, Anthony?"

"Not a smile."

"Then I'll go wherever you please."

"Will you?"

"Yes," she said.

"Why do you keep your eyes closed, Dinah?" he asked. "Are you seeing the other fellow's face?"

"What other face?"

"The one for whom you need all the money. What would he think if he knew what's in your mind now? What would he do, Dinah?"

"Laugh, I suppose," she answered.

"Is that all there is to it?"

She opened her eyes after this long moment. The intense blue of them under the black of her hair was a perennial surprise. But she did not speak.

He parked the car among the crowd of them at the side of the villa, and walked around the corner of the great house with her toward the entrance.

Someone called out behind them. Harry Calliver and De Briggis and two or three girls came hurrying up, and they all went into the house with much chattering and laughing.

Then Nancy Ormonde picked him up with her eyes and brought him to her side. She was dressed in a rose-colored affair, with the yellow lustre of the lining shining through the sheer outer material.

"I like your dress," said Newcomen.

"I'm glad you like the *dress*," said Nancy, looking at it and then smiling at him.

"Nancy, what a relief you are!" he said. "To be with you, why, it's like walking out of darkness into daylight. You're so frank. Where's our host?"

"Poor Franco! He's occupied for a moment, the servants say. I suppose with some of his silly police work. The old house doesn't have the right sort of life unless he's in it, do you think?"

"No, it doesn't," said Newcomen. "All these old pictures... Why do people ever go in for painted flowers?"

A voice spoke to Nancy and hurried by. Newcomen turned his head and saw Bertelli gliding through the crowd.

"Why should Bertelli go past you at such a rate?" he asked. "You haven't been harsh to him, have you?"

"You know how Italians are," she said. "They're always thinking around a corner before one gets to it."

"Has Bertelli simply been forehanded about it?" asked Newcomen, laughing.

Nicholas Decker appeared beside them, saying: "Bertelli? Have you been talking about the Bertelli news?"

Neither of them spoke to him. They did not smile either, but Nicholas Decker was not easily affronted. His eyes and his mustache shone with an equal brilliance, and his color had been heightened by cocktails. He kept laughing as he talked.

"Aldo has struck it rich. Really paying his debts. I know of twenty or thirty thousand lire that he's cleared off. Astonishing fellow, eh? Where would a Bertelli be getting so much money? What bank would trust him? What relative has any money? Where has he been gambling? It's a mystery, eh?"

He picked up a little stiletto
which could not have been
long in the ground.

THEY GOT rid of Decker, and a moment later big Lucardo came
panting into the house, shaking hands, pouring out greetings.
His party had gathered a good headway. People were wandering
through the formal garden in front of the house, and here and
there in the big rooms. All the invited guests had come, and a
few friends who refused to be overlooked, for Lucardo opened
his house in this fashion hardly more than once a year. He was
made exclusive on the one hand by his ancient name and on the

other by his poverty. He hailed Newcomen, and got him into the study. The floorspace was small, but the ceiling was as lofty as the largest salon on the ground floor.

"This is like a chapel," said Newcomen. "Leads your thoughts upward, doesn't it?"

"Upward?" echoed Lucardo blankly, looking at the white stucco angels who were stuck to the ceiling. "Ah, well! I wanted to thank you for the letter, *Signor* Newcomen, and for the stiletto, as well. What a sharp blade! What steel!"

"What letter?" asked Newcomen. "And what stiletto?"

The *marchese* did not seem to hear the remark. He rambled on: "We have lost the secret of making that beautiful steel. Mass production is good enough for pins and needles, but daggers are another matter. The handmade thing is still the best in a pinch. Here is a dagger that could be used as well by a child as by a grown man. Only find the proper place, and the blade will do the rest!"

"My dear *marchese*," said Newcomen, "the dagger looks like business. But do you mind telling me what you're talking about?"

"Ah, well," said Lucardo, "I knew you would admire fine steel. There was blood on it, my friend. And I have just received a report that the blood is of the type of Decker's. Shall we get back to the others? But do remember that when you have a little spare time I should like to talk to you."

"It would be an honor and a pleasure," said Newcomen.

He went out with the *marchese*, and a moment later saw Bertelli lingering from group to group.

The Italian joined him in a corner of the music room.

Newcomen said: "I've brought some cash with me, *Signor* Bertelli. So suppose we have the name at once?"

Bertelli nodded and smiled.

"You shall have it at once, but we must not part immediately. It is proper enough for us to be seen chatting, I hope, even if the murderer comes in and sees us," he said.

"The killer is here?" asked Newcomen.

"By all means!" said Bertelli. "I wondered, for instance, if you have made a guess about the sex of the murderer, *signore?*"

"A stiletto," said Newcomen, "could be used as well by a woman as by a man."

"Ah? A stiletto?" said Bertelli. "Do you know it was a stiletto?"

"Do *you?*" answered Newcomen.

"I saw the blow struck!" replied the Italian, setting his jaw hard and nodding.

"That's the sort of testimony that counts in a courtroom," said Newcomen.

"It will never be given in a courtroom!" answered Bertelli.

"Come, come!" said Newcomen. "You don't expect me to pay for testimony that can't be given to a judge?"

"I offered to give you the name," said Bertelli sharply. "I didn't offer to prove the case in a law court. I offer you a name which will surprise you so much that you will understand at once that I have told you the truth."

"Why should it surprise me?" asked Newcomen.

Bertelli parted his lips in a laugh that made no sound.

"The question is," said Bertelli, "are you prepared to pay for that name?"

"You were an eyewitness?" asked Newcomen.

"Yes,"said the Italian, bowing a little as though he were acknowledging a bit of praise.

"You can show the motives behind the killing?" persisted Newcomen.

"I can, *signore.*"

"But you will not talk in a witness box?"

"I believe," said Bertelli, "that the flesh of a Bertelli is just as mortal as the flesh of a Thomas Decker."

"So we let it go at that?"

"Will you pay or will you not?" demanded Bertelli.

"Two hundred and fifty thousand lire!" murmured Newcomen.

"Exactly that sum," snapped Bertelli, reddening.

"Very well," said Newcomen suddenly. "I'll pay."

Here a servant, approaching in haste, called: *"Signor* Bertelli, a very urgent telephone message for you. Very urgent, *signore!"*

"I come back at once," said Bertelli, and hurried from the room.

Newcomen, scowling after him for an instant, suddenly followed. The music room was left to the chatter of a half dozen people.

The sun had been pouring red through the western windows for some time, casting a tremulous pattern of leaf shadows from the climbing vines which twisted up among the window-bars. Now those shadows blurred suddenly. The light grew both more red and more dim, and then a soft wall of shadow washed across the world as the sun sank.

It was just at this moment that someone began to cry out at the top of his voice. His words could not be understood at once. A rumor flew out before them like an echo around a loud sound.

Aldo Bertelli had been found dead at the telephone in the study of the *marchese.*

Lucardo was not present at the moment. Newcomen and Nicholas Decker were in the study with the butler, staring at the body of Bertelli, sprawled across the desk, his left hand gripping the telephone receiver, and a spot of blood extending from a narrow slit in the back of his coat. He was wearing white linen, and the red of the stain was very clear.

Newcomen picked up the receiver and spoke into the phone.

A woman's voice was calling excitedly. *"Signore! Signor* Bertelli!"

Newcomen looked down at the narrow rat face of Bertelli, whose eyes were still half open. He seemed to be pressing his ear against the desk to listen, like a doctor, for the beating of a heart.

"Who is speaking?" asked Newcomen. *"Signor* Bertelli was called away."

"But I was talking to him this moment. I am Teresa, his maid and the message said I was to telephone to him at once, because he wished to say something terribly urgent. And then he groaned... *Signore,* what has happened?"

"Be calm, Teresa," said Newcomen. "Who spoke to you?"

"There was no name. But I was told to telephone instantly to the Villa Lucardo and ask for my *signore.*"

"You spoke with *Signor* Bertelli?" asked Newcomen.

"Yes, *signore.* Only three words—and then he groaned and said nothing more."

"You will hear about everything presently," said Newcomen. "That is all."

He rang off.

"Do you see?" Nicholas Decker was saying. "In exactly the same spot and exactly the same sort of a wound as the one that killed Thomas. The same murderer has killed Bertelli! But how could the same person wish to kill the two of them? What did *they* have in common?"

"They had your friendship in common," said Newcomen coldly.

He stepped back to the middle of the room and began to look over it, calmly.

"Both the doors were open," said Nicholas Decker. "You noticed that? Both doors were open, and yet Bertelli was stabbed right there, at the desk, where twenty people might have seen the thing happen from the hall."

"I noticed that," agreed Newcomen. He turned his head and listened, for a moment, to the babble of voices, the muttering of running feet through the house. From outside the villa he heard motors roar and whine as people who were more timid than curious rushed away from the unlucky house.

"But think of it again!" insisted Nicholas Decker. "To step in here behind poor Aldo and knife him, deliberately... The person who did that had a nerve as cold as yours, Newcomen."

Here Decker stopped short and laid a hand over his mouth, bright mustaches and all, while he stared at Newcomen, his eyes great with his suspicion.

"Yes," said Newcomen carelessly. "A very cool or a very frightened fellow did this trick."

He turned to the butler. "Who told you that *Signor* Bertelli was wanted on the telephone?" he asked.

"The telephone told me, *signore*. That is to say, it rang, and when I answered, a woman said that she had a terribly great need of speaking to *Signor* Bertelli at once."

"Did she give her name?" asked Newcomen.

"No, *signore*. There was something in her voice that made me go at once to call *Signor* Bertelli."

"Someone knew that I was speaking to Bertelli, just then," said Newcomen.

"Pardon me, *signore?*" echoed the amazed butler.

"Nothing," said Newcomen.

He turned abruptly away and stared at the wall opposite the desk of the *marchese*. A picture of an old Tuscan scene hung there, a villa on a hill with muleteers driving their loaded animals slowly up the bending of the road toward the great house, and a bridge in the foreground, with half of a village church.

Something glinted at the foot of the wall. Newcomen leaned and picked it up between his thumb and forefinger.

"It was left behind, this time," he said, and showed to Nicholas Decker the little stiletto, now bathed in blood, with a large dark drop of red adhering to the point.

Newcomen placed the weapon on the blotter of the desk. The paper began to soak up a spreading red stain.

"Where's Lucardo? He ought to be on hand," said Newcomen, "with all this confusion going on."

"Lucardo?" gasped Nicholas Decker. "I wonder if I have the answer! Lucardo who said that poor Tom *gave* him back his promissory notes that night—Lucardo who invites Bertelli here to this party and then—Lucardo who owes so much money that he must be ready to do murder... I have it; it's true! Find Lucardo and you find the double murderer. Get him! Wait a moment and I'll prove the point. You won't find Lucardo; he isn't here because he's taken to his heels. Poor Aldo! Stabbed in the back by that fat fool. Find Lucardo. Find the *marchese!*"

"Wait," called Newcomen. "Be quiet, you fool!"

But Nicholas Decker already had broken out from the room, and his voice went shouting through the halls: "Find Lucardo. Find the *marchese*. Murder! Catch Lucardo. Murder!"

NEWCOMEN, NOW that the roaring voice of Nicholas Decker was bellowing through the house, shrugged his shoulders and turned back to the desk, where he leaned for some time over the stiletto, waiting.

But the *marchese* did not appear.

By this time a large part of the guests had hurried from the place: those who remained were held together by a growing wonder and a sort of horrified delight such as that which gossips feel when a real social crime looms within their ken. For Lucardo had disappeared from the villa completely. A search organized on the spot combed the big house from top to cellar, but not a trace of him was found.

Nicholas Decker seemed to rejoice in this disappearance. He took on himself the air of a prophet and talked with such excitement that he almost forgot to sleek his mustaches. Newcomen said to him: "After all, what earthly reason can there be for the *marchese* to stab a fellow like Bertelli? An unimportant rat like Bertelli!"

Decker cried: "Blackmail! But Lucardo can't stand being bled so long. He strikes back."

"In his own house," said Newcomen, "when it was filled with

people? In his own study, with two doors wide open on a hall where people might be walking back and forth at any time?"

"In his own house—because nobody will suspect the host," said Decker. "In his own study—because notice that his study opens on the east, and the sunset light from the west pours the room full of dimness. Neat! Oh, Franco was very neat about it! And then he heard my voice bawling out his name and accusing him, and a panic takes hold of him. He sees that the devil has started on his trail, and he runs for his life. Fat men are easily frightened."

"How clearly you've worked it all out," murmured Newcomen, watching him. "What a good brain you have for crime!"

Nicholas Decker was stopped short by this remark. He regarded Newcomen through narrowed eyes, for an instant, and then he answered: "I? Well, a man has what God gives him!" But afterward he went quickly away.

The police, arriving a few moments later, found Newcomen in the study with the dead man, studying the handle of the stiletto with a large reading glass. The butler looked on from the shadows of a corner.

"Notice," said Newcomen, "that there are no fingerprints on the hilt. Here where the blood spurted, it soaked through some sort of cloth, and left the checking of a very fine-grained material..."

The commissary himself was in the room.

"*Signore,*" he said, "your observations are invaluable. To have the assistance of your eyes, what would we not give? But in the meantime, if we may be permitted to go ahead in our own stupid, unassisted way..."

Newcomen went out to his car, and found Dinah Moore already waiting in it. She pulled her skirt aside and drew the fullness of it over her knees as he climbed in.

"What do you think, Dinah?" he asked as he started the car.

She made one of her usual pauses before she answered: "I think you're very tired, Anthony."

"I? Tired?" he said. "Oh, that's stuff. I'm not tired."

The remark irritated him. He drove hard and fast.

He got her to the *villino*. When he saw her to her door, he said: "I'll give you a ring, shortly. You know, Dinah, I'd give a good deal to know just what's in your mind now."

"Would you?" she asked. "But you wouldn't like it, Anthony. Good night."

When he reached the house, the huge empty dimness of the hall arrested him.

"Lights," he said to the butler. "I want plenty of lights tonight. Everywhere. All over the house. You understand? Burn some of the darkness out of this place."

He went up to his room, stepping quickly because slow motions caused his knees to sag a little under the weight of his own body, and this annoyed him. For his mind to be blanketed with a mist of weariness did not matter so much, because he could fight that off; but the sense of physical weakness told him how long he had gone without real sleep, and he was alarmed.

As he opened the door of his own apartment, the air from an open window pushed toward him, whispering. The breath of it was qualified faintly by the cigarette smoke of that same day. He paused, stopped by the dimness of the room, for no lights had been turned on in it and the starlight made only one dim step past the windows, only enough to show him, in the easy chair beside the open window, the bulk of a big man who was sitting at ease, perfectly reposed, his legs stretched out before him.

Newcomen closed the door behind him and stretched out his hand for the switch.

"Ah, Lucardo," he said, "I was expecting you, with half of my mind."

Then he turned on the lights.

ON THE morning of the sixth day after the death of Thomas Decker. Newcomen came down in the light of dawn to the *villino*.

He threw a pebble up through the open French windows behind the balcony, and Hans came out and looked at him with a sort of patient hatred. Then Dinah came into the dark rectangle of a window, looking tall in the long sweep of her dressing gown. She looked down at Newcomen as silently as the dog.

"Will you come down?" he asked.

"Have you had any sleep?" she answered.

"Will you come down?" he repeated.

"Yes," she said, and disappeared.

He walked up and down on the terrace, breathing deeply to get the fumes of cigarette smoke out of his lungs, until the girl appeared with the black shadow of the dog gliding behind her.

"We'll have breakfast out here in moment," she said. "Could you eat some toast—very dry?"

"No, I couldn't eat it," admitted Newcomen. "Do I look as bad as that?"

She considered him gravely and thoroughly, and said nothing.

"Say something," commanded Newcomen.

"It's the sixth day," said the girl. "But can you last out till tomorrow?"

"What will happen tomorrow?" he asked.

"Before he died, Tom Decker was very nervous," she said. "So was Aldo Bertelli—very nervous yesterday. And you're nervous today. Very."

"Does that mean that I am about to die? Am I to follow them?"

She allowed the question to answer itself.

The big tray arrived and was placed on one of the iron garden tables.

"I've been doing some thinking," Newcomen said. "Want to know about what?"

Dinah looked away from him across that most beautiful valley in the world. Her eyes forgot the Duomo, the towers.

"Or do you already know?" he asked.

"I know," she said, nodding.

"Well, what have I been thinking about just now?" he demanded.

"About me, Anthony," she said.

"What have I been thinking?"

"That I am beautiful."

"Am I wrong?"

The sleeves of her dress were thin chiffon, cut very wide. She folded her arms like a Chinaman, with the hands inside the sleeves.

"Go on and tell me, Dinah," he insisted. "Am I wrong?"

"No," she said. "Your thinking makes me so."

"You told me at Impruneta that I'd never know real love."

"I was wrong," she said.

"But is it the big thing?" he asked. "I mean, has the golden lightning hit me? Do I see the stars at noon?"

"Yes," she said.

"Well, a thing like that is deathless, isn't it?" asked Newcomen.

"Yes, deathless," she said.

"But do I mean anything to you?" he asked.

"Yes," she answered.

"How much?"

"Everything," she said.

"Say that again," he directed.

"I love you, Anthony," she said.

After a moment he asked: "What was I wishing all last night?"

"That you'd never seen me," she said.

"Dinah!"

"Yes, Anthony?"

"What's the matter with us?"

"It's a beautiful sort of wretchedness, isn't it?" she asked.

"Why do you smile like that?" he asked. "We're not saying a sad good-bye."

"Aren't we?" said Dinah.

"I don't follow this," he said. "Why don't I take you in my arms? You would not care, would you?"

"No," she said.

"You'd like it, wouldn't you, Dinah?"

"Yes," she said.

"We'd both like it more than anything in the world, wouldn't we?" asked Newcomen.

SHE LOOKED at him and smiled again.

"Yes," she said.

"What are you reading in my face, Dinah? Ugly words?"

"Yes," she said.

"But in spite of them, you'd have me? No matter what the ugliness is?"

"Yes," she said.

"Then what stands between us, Dinah?" he asked.

She kept on reading his face like a page of small print.

"What's between us?" he repeated.

"A dead man, I suppose," she answered.

After a moment of staring, he took out a handkerchief and scrubbed his wet face.

"Sit down and eat something," said Newcomen.

"I don't want anything to eat, Anthony."

"Sit down and eat something," he commanded.

She sat down behind the iron table. He watched her hands as she poured coffee and hot milk. She raised the cup and tasted the drink. The heat of it puckered her forehead.

"Actually, you're hardly more than a baby," said Newcomen.

She looked up at him.

"Eat some of the toast, too," said Newcomen.

She broke a piece of it. He listened to the crunching. He watched her swallowing. When she paused, he said: "Try one of those peaches, too."

She peeled it like a European, with knife and fork. He watched the small slices disappear.

"If I love you in the great way—knocking the sun out of the sky and letting the stars come out—like that, if I love you, all I want is you. Isn't that true?"

She leaned back in her chair.

"Yes," she said.

"Then tell me what keeps me from falling on my knees beside you, Dinah, and thanking God for you; and putting my hands on you; and holding you so that when you speak I can feel your voice and not care what you're saying because there is only one thought in our flesh; and nothing to breathe except the blue of the sky. That's the way it ought to be with us, isn't it?"

"Yes," she said.

The dimness in her eyes collected in tears that rolled slowly down her face. Newcomen lighted a cigarette.

"When did you begin loving me?" he asked.

"Well—always," she said.

"There wasn't anyone before, not even a ghost?"

"No," she said.

"You expect me to believe that?"

"No, Anthony."

"Well?"

"You don't think there could be some sort of hope, do you? For things to be better, I mean? Some small sort of a hope that I could hold onto?"

"You mean some sort of hope that we might find happiness together, after all?"

"Yes."

"You mean," said Newcomen, "a hope that we might be married and have children and all that?"

"Yes."

"No there's no hope of that at all," he told her.

"You wouldn't marry me, Anthony?"

"No."

SHE CLOSED her eyes. He watched her for a time. The sun had swung around the corner of the house until it lay across her knees. Her lap was filled with rosy fire that stained her hands.

"But, Dinah, you don't *expect* me to marry you, do you?" he asked.

"No," she said.

"With what I know, you don't expect that, do you?" he repeated.

"No," she whispered. "From the moment you found the green tassel, you were more than half sure that I was guilty. Isn't that true?"

"Yes."

"And you bought my time for a week simply because you had a ghost of a hope that if you came to know me you would know for sure? You wanted to try me, wasn't that it?"

"Yes," said Newcomen. "Will you forget that for a while. We might go off some place together. Would you do that?"

"Yes," she said.

"Then pack your things and get out of Florence, now!" he commanded.

She started up from the chair, crying out: "Will you go with me, now?"

"What do you think?" he asked.

"No. You'll stay here," she answered, sinking down in the chair again.

"You know that, don't you?" he asked.

"Yes," she said, closing her eyes again. She made an effort and then spoke with her eyes still shut.

"Where shall I go?" she asked.

"Somewhere up in the mountains. You know why?"

"Yes. Everything seems cleaner there."

"You start for Merano. I'll go after you tomorrow. Some time tomorrow I'll start. You wire back the name of the hotel you're staying in."

"Anthony, will you come with me?"

"No," he said.

"For sweet pity's sake, will you come with me, Anthony?"

He threw down his cigarette and stamped on it.

"No," he said.

He turned his back and walked rapidly away, down the bend of the driveway, with the gravel crunching noisily under his feet.

HUGH CHURCHILL, since the coming of his new master, had formed the pleasant habit of lying late in bed, a privilege which he relished almost as much as he despised the carelessness of Newcomen which permitted such indolence in the people who served him. On this morning, the seventh since the death of Thomas Decker, the secretary took a good breakfast, propped on the pillows which the second butler assiduously piled for him, and when he came to his second cup of coffee he opened *La Nazione,* lighted a cigarette, and stared at the headlines, while the fumes from the cigarette rose in a wavering line, unregarded.

The smoldering fire in the tobacco touched and scorched his fingers before he dropped the cigarette. His coffee grew cold. Still he read, and anger gathered slowly in his breast as he realized that news had come from the Villa Oliviera and passed into the world before a whisper of it had touched his sensitive ears.

La Nazione carried the news in a big way and in much detail. In brief, the story it told was that *Signor* Newcomen, the rich American who was the owner of the famous old Villa Oliviera, did not believe that Marchese Lucardo, now hunted everywhere through the land for the murder of Aldo Bertelli, was guilty of the crime. Instead, he put his faith in a new clue which was in his hands and which he declared would turn out to be the trap which must inevitably cause the capture of the real criminal.

Hugh Churchill, wriggling his shoulders into perfect comfort against the pillows, at last lighted a cigarette which he smoked in deep inhalations, while he reviewed the main points of the story with meticulous care, and all the while lights of malicious interest flickered in his eyes like small fish in dingy water.

"It lies in a little empty phial," said the detailed report in the newspaper, "one of those small glass bottles of a well-known type which are used for aspirin. And the clue itself is simply a very fine linen thread, considerably frayed. There is significance in the thread, however; there is one touch of vital interest, and *Signor* Newcomen permitted us to stare at it through an enlarging glass. Seen in this manner, the texture of the thread is much enlarged, and at one end of it appears a red stain. The red stain is blood, and it is the blood of the murdered man, Aldo Bertelli!"

Of the finding of the thread, the newspaper said: "When *Signor* Newcomen, one of the first people to enter the room where the dead man sat bowed over the desk of Marchese Lucardo, picked up the blood-dripping stiletto which had been plunged into Bertelli's back, he found on the hilt of it, stuck to the crevice where the handle joins its narrow guard, this tiny thread on which a human life may now depend. According to *Signor* Newcomen, a life does actually depend upon it and the murderer is now in the hands of the law, to all intents and purposes, as literally as though he stood on the trap, with the hangman's rope knotted around his neck! In brief, it is the theory of *Signor* Newcomen that the killer, unwilling to risk fingerprints on the hilt of the dagger, too hurried to put on a glove, wrapped a handkerchief around the handle of the knife before striking the fatal blow. But the single thread caught in the crevice, and the thread will be fatal to the criminal!

"The reason why it might be fatal, Newcomen had enlarged with much detailed clarity. In New York, not long before, there was a murder of singular brutality. A woman was found maltreated and strangled in the bathtub of her apartment. Every clue had been removed by the murderer with the possible exception of a small piece of twine which lay beneath her dead body. That piece of twine had been enough to lead the police to the killer.'

"In this case, we have not a piece of twine but a meagre thread pulled from a bit of handkerchief linen," Newcomen had told the reporter. "The smallness does not matter. The microscope makes up the difference; it turns a hairsbreadth into a handful. There is only needed an expert in the field with an expert's experience and knowledge to interpret the facts for us; and already I have wired to Professor Emile Cardeaux. He is on his way to Florence from Paris. He will arrive here on the eleven o'clock train tonight. By eleven-thirty the bit of evidence will be in his hands. It may take a day or two, or even a week, for him to arrange the facts. But soon everything will be made clear. The bit of thread becomes the executioner's rope. By degrees it is learned who made the handkerchief; from that point, we easily discover what person present in the house of the *marchese* on the day of the murder had such a handkerchief in his possession. And after that, the end follows on quickly."

WHEN CHURCHILL had finished his reading, he lay passive in the enjoyment of another cigarette, smiling to himself before he rose and commenced his bath. Afterward, he went to Newcomen and found him in the orangerie behind the villa. Where the sun slanted down on the gravel, it shone like marble, but all the shadows were blackened with dew.

Newcomen walked up and down among the great red pots and the twisted little deformities of the orange and lemon trees. The commissary of police himself was with him, walking back and forth. Now he stopped by the central fountain and stared at the water lilies which were wide open in the sun and still closed in the shadow.

Hugh Churchill, after the manner of one who enjoys himself with deliberation, took note of this as he walked slowly toward his employer, but it was the face of Newcomen himself that he studied with the greatest relish, for every day of the past week had cut itself into the flesh of Newcomen like a long year of life. The strain in his forehead and the underpainting of purple around his eyes made him look like an actor made up for a tragic part; and all was drawn so hard with tension that he looked brittle.

The conversation which passed between Newcomen and the commissary, the secretary would have given his soul to overhear, but he dared not come within earshot. He had to dally in the distance, while in fact the agent of the police was saying: "But although we appreciate the subtlety of your management in this affair, *Signor* Newcomen, the fact is that we must not allow private hands to take total charge of a case of this importance."

Here it was that Newcomen stopped short in his pacing and said, bluntly: "There is no Professor Emile Cardeaux of Paris. And he is not coming here. And the thread in the aspirin bottle is simply a bit of line thread cut off a spool. And nobody, so far as I know, can derive anything from it."

"But *signore!* The newspapers…"

"The newspapers," said Newcomen, "make fools of us so often that it's only fair for us to make fools of them, now and again. Don't you agree? They've printed the stuff I told them. And as a result, I'm angling a long line with a barbed hook on the end of it. *Signor il Commissario,* I think that I have more than a ghost of a chance of catching the murderer tonight. Do you understand?"

The commissary thought once and parted his lips to speak; he thought again and decided not to waste his voice on opinions.

"If you succeed, *signore,*" he said, "you have my compliments.

On the couch sat Dinah Moore, with her hands
interlaced in her lap, staring calmly at them.

"Stand up," ordered Lucardo, "stand up
without touching your handbag."

If you fail. I shall have to call on you in an unpleasant official manner. Good-bye!"

And he went off with a quick, stiff, military step, like a man marching in a parade.

Churchill came up at once, and Newcomen said impatiently, with hardly an upward glance: "Yes, Churchill? Yes?"

"I wanted to talk to you for a few minutes," said Churchill.

"Sorry. One minute will have to do," answered Newcomen. "What is it?"

"The Marchese Lucardo," said Churchill. "What is he worth to you?"

"The poor devil is being hunted all over the country," said Newcomen.

"So I wondered," said Churchill, "what it would be worth to the police if I told them that he was within a hundred feet of the place where I am now standing."

"Meaning what?" asked Newcomen.

"In your house!" said Churchill. "I wondered what that would be worth to the police?"

"Churchill, I'm going to shut your mouth," said Newcomen. "How much money do I have to spend to choke you off?"

The scorn and disgust behind this question left Churchill completely unmoved. He said: "If you consider buying me off, we ought to talk about what it would mean to me. Not simply letting Lucardo have your protection, but then there is the great loss to me in that I'll have to leave your employment."

"Does that follow?" asked Newcomen. "Yes, I suppose it does. What do you suggest?"

"Security, plus freedom," replied Churchill. "That I could secure at a low price. A thousand lire a month? That's not much, surely. That works out at twelve thousand a year. Five per cent, suppose we say? That brings it to about two hundred and forty thousand as a capital sum. You see, when you divide that by the rate of exchange it's not very much, is it? And for that. I walk out and leave you at peace, Tony."

Newcomen rubbed a hand swiftly across his forehead. His mouth twitched. After a time he was able to say: "Have you any idea why I should spend a small fortune on account of Lucardo?"

"My dear Tony," said the secretary, with his smile, "all I know is that you're willing to do the spending. I have no right to dip into possibilities and probabilities. What assistance you have given to Lucardo or why he is necessary to you—that is not my affair, unless you wish me to guess."

"I don't wish you to guess," said Newcomen. "Good morning."

"Good morning," said Churchill. "Beautiful day, isn't it?"

And he went off with a light step, turning his head from side to side so that he would miss none of the beauty of the morning.

RAIN COMES to Florence out of the southwest. This day, shortly after noon, Monte Morella was wearing the *capella,* which means a storm, and then the clouds washed up out of the southwestern horizon and came in a long, smooth deluge over the Arno valley. San Domenico was covered in the middle of the afternoon by the cloud shadows, and in the early evening a fine rain began which increased in the early night to a trampling downpour. A pull of the wind toward the north interrupted the steady rain, which began to come in gusts with intervals during which patches of stars were visible. In one of those clearing moments Marchese Lucardo and Newcomen reached the front door of the *villino.*

Lucardo flashed a single ray from his pocket torch across the windows. They winked back with empty black eyes. Newcomen took the key from his pocket.

"Give it to me," said Lucardo, so softly that Newcomen hardly could hear him.

"What's the matter?" asked Newcomen, still fingering the key.

"It's better for me to have it," answered Lucardo, and he took possession.

He did not fit it at once into the lock, but remained for a moment leaning his head close to the door as though he were listening.

Then he stepped back, saying: "You got no message today from her?"

"From whom?" asked Newcomen.

"From Dinah Moore. No telegram? No telephone from long distance?"

"Nothing," said Newcomen.

"Do you think you ever will see her face again?" asked the *marchese.*

"No," said Newcomen.

"And so you are sick?"

"Lucardo, what I feel doesn't matter."

"Tell me one thing," said the *marchese.* "If it is true that the lovely lady—ah, my friend, how lovely she is!—but if it is true that she has gone on out of your ken, would you help the law to recapture her?"

"I'll help the law," said Newcomen, "with every bit of money or brains that I have."

"Good!" said Lucardo. "Then we can go inside."

He began to fit the key into the lock, which took some time. He managed everything so carefully that not a sound was made in setting the door ajar.

"Wait till the wind dies a little," whispered the *marchese* over his shoulder. "Then step in quickly behind me."

But he remained waiting for the fall of the wind during several long minutes. At last the rain came down with a rush, and the wind no longer beat against the side of the house. At that moment Lucardo pushed the door ajar and stepped inside with one of those sudden, light movements of which he was capable. Newcomen followed.

The door closed soundlessly. A mere whisper of the wind preceded them through the darkness like a scurrying of mice.

The *marchese* did not move at once. He remained for a considerable moment close to the door, and Newcomen spent the interval trying to penetrate the darkness with his ears and his eyes. The black interior came alive before his face, whirling into vague images, but nothing was real.

The sweet, stale odor that invades a closed house lived in the air, a ghost of cookery, of floor polish, of dead flowers, of perfumes.

Then Newcomen saw in fact a dim form drifting before him. He felt the shock first; then he realized that it was Lucardo, proceeding noiselessly across the hall. He followed.

One ray from the *marchese's* flashlight splintered on the mirror at the side of the hall. It slashed across the lower steps of the stairway. Pace by pace. Lucardo mounted through the blackness. Now and again he paused. There was no whisper from his clothes and no creaking from his shoes. Newcomen found himself stifling as he held his breath.

They gained the upper level. The hand of Lucardo sounded faintly as he passed it over the stucco of the wall. Right through the wall he seemed to fade out; Newcomen followed through the open door.

Then through the darkness Newcomen heard distinctly a sound of breathing incredibly quick, as a man breathes after he has been running hard; something scratched on the tiled floor; and then the torch of Lucardo plunged a broad cone of brilliance into the room.

IT SHOWED the eyes of Hans first, red and phosphorescent as he stood on guard in front of the davenport. On the couch sat Dinah Moore with her hands interlaced in her lap, staring calmly at them.

"Speak to the dog, *signorina*," said Lucardo. "I think the brute is about to rush at me."

She said something which Newcomen did not hear, and the dog slipped down to a crouching position.

"Stand up," said Lucardo. "If you please, stand up, without touching your handbag."

She did, in fact, put out her hand to the purse, but after a moment she rose. She was wearing a light travelling dress with a white collar that framed and set off the youth in her face. It should have accented also the least pallor, but Newcomen could detect nothing pinched or drawn about her mouth. She seemed entirely calm and watchful.

"Open the purse, *Signor* Newcomen, if you please," directed Lucardo.

Newcomen picked up the purse, hesitated, and then passed it unopened to the *marchese.*

"Will you keep an eye on her, closely?" asked Lucardo.

"Yes. Closely," said Newcomen.

Lucardo gave his attention to the bag.

"Why?" asked Newcomen of the girl.

She smiled at him and shook her head.

"You didn't leave Florence at all?" he insisted.

"Yes."

"When did you return?"

"Very soon," she answered.

Hans jumped on the davenport, and stood with his head as high as her shoulder, eyeing Newcomen.

"Down, Hans!" she commanded.

"Let him be," said Newcomen. "He's about all you have to take care of you in the world."

The dog had not moved.

"Do you know that?" insisted Newcomen.

As she had done so often before, she answered his question with something in her eyes, but her words were: "He obeys you a little now. Have you noticed that?"

He looked at the big dog, and saw the tail of Hans slowly wag as though he were making an involuntary concession to friendliness. Newcomen felt a strange shock of pleasure.

The *marchese* said: "My dear *Signor* Newcomen, will you be interested in the contents of this purse? We find our charming lady sitting alone in the dark with the dog—but no, not quite alone. She has a companion who can protect her better than any man. Do you see?"

He held upon the flat of his hand a small automatic. The stub nose of it showed a brutally large mouth.

"Loaded," said the *marchese*, weighing it. "Loaded and ready. Dear *signorina*, for whom was the gun waiting here in the dark?"

Instead of answering, she looked at Newcomen.

"Well?" asked Newcomen.

"Do you think there's any use in explanations—from me?" she asked.

He shrugged his shoulders. Lucardo remarked: "If you'll stay here with her. *Signor* Newcomen, and watch her carefully while I look a bit through the house..."

Newcomen took out his own flashlight and snapped on a ray from it.

"I'll stay here with her," he answered. "But are you sure that you want to go through the house alone?"

"It will be better," said Lucardo. "We old bird hunters know how to move silently even over dead leaves, you know."

He turned at the door, saying this, and laughed back at Newcomen, whose flashlight glanced across the humid, shining face and the gleam of the eyes; then Lucardo disappeared, moving as softly as his promise. Newcomen turned the flashlight down toward the feet of the girl. The darkness swallowed the rest of her except a sort of breathing warmth and the thin, clean odor of the perfume which he had noticed before.

"DO YOU trust the *marchese?*" she asked. "He might be a great brown fox. Did you see his eyes when he stood there in the doorway?"

"I saw his eyes," said Newcomen. "And I trust *him.*"

"But not me?" she asked.

He put his arms about her. The dog, still standing on the davenport, sniffed at their faces.

"Dinah," he said, "are you guilty?"

She was silent. "Answer me!" commanded Newcomen.

She strained up on tiptoe and kissed him. With her hands she bent his head and kissed his mouth. He trembled.

"Well," he said, "in spite of Lucardo I won't keep you... Stand away from me, Dinah."

She kissed him again. He pulled down her arms and held both her wrists in his left hand. The weight of her body swayed in against his arm.

"Anthony!" she whispered.

"I love you," said Newcomen. "I love you! That's why I give you the chance to get out and away. But if I find you again, I swear that I'll turn you over to the law. They can jam you into prison and mug you and fingerprint you and then hang you at their pleasure. Now get away from me!"

He turned his back. It seemed to Newcomen that she remained there close to him, and that same sense of the inexpressible warm breath of life enveloped him. Then he heard a light scratching noise toward the door. When he turned, he knew that the girl and the dog had gone, and he was amazed by the shock this gave him.

Afterward he got hold of himself by degrees. The thought of Lucardo was the point at which his wits began to rally. It would be hard to explain to the *marchese* why he had allowed the girl to go.

He went to the window. Two or three stars were stuck in the upper pane of it like imprisoned fireflies. The cypresses outside stood up like slender, black candle flames. Like things that were meant for the shedding of darkness, he thought.

Then someone in the room above shouted; footfalls raced; two gunshots banged against his eardrums.

He saw a picture in the black of his mind of Dinah Moore with two bullet wounds enlarging and ruining her mouth—the whole centre of her face smashed in. Somehow he thought of that picture as he raced out of the living room and up the stairs, and into the room above.

A pocket torch lying on the floor showed a glistening space of red tiles, the feet of the piano, a couch beyond, a big old oil jar filled with some sort of long-stemmed white flowers, and on the wall a painting of Judith walking with the head, swinging her sword in her stride. A dim, rather worthless old picture, but it had a special meaning to the first glance Newcomen gave that room.

With his own torch he found something else, at once. Over by the feet of a corner console lay Lucardo, flat on his back, his arms outstretched and blood on his face! A gun glimmered on the tiles not far from him. A stride away stood the house safe, with the door of it open and a stack of papers spilled out on the floor.

Newcomen jumped back into the hallway, groaning, and jerked his light down the stairs, down the hall. He made himself stop breathing, put a hand against the wall, and listened. As the uproar of his mind quieted, the steady downpouring of the rain beat gradually into his ears.

Instead of attempting some blind gesture of pursuit, he turned back into the room of Dinah to the fallen *marchese.* The wound was on the forehead above the left eye, a small tear of flesh that did not look in the least like a place where a bullet could have gone through; but bullets can do strange things. He slid his hand up under the coat of Lucardo. The belly muscles, instead of being relaxed, were tensed under the soft, thick sheathing of outer fat.

Higher, he pressed his index finger down over the heart; the throb of it answered him instantly!

Lucardo sat up an instant later. He got to his knees and to his feet. Then, with a handkerchief pressed against the wound above his eye, he leaned on Newcomen, saying: "Did I hit him, *signore?* There by the door—is there blood?"

NEWCOMEN FLOODED the tiles with the light from his torch.

"There's no blood," he said.

"You speak in your country of buck fever," said the *marchese*. "But for an old hunter like me to start running at my target instead of standing still and hitting it—can you believe that, my friend?"

"It was a gun, Lucardo?" asked Newcomen, with a sudden, vast relief. "It wasn't a woman?"

"I don't know," said the *marchese*. "When I came up to this room, I thought I saw a flicker, a ray of light under the edge of the door: but when I pushed the door open there was nothing inside it except the open door of that safe and the stuff spilling out on the floor. That was all. I came over here toward the safe and felt something move behind me. When I turned, before I'd centered the flashlight on it, the thing was slipping through the doorway. I shouted out a warning to halt. At the same time I started running. Ah, that is where I made myself a fool! As I ran, I fired twice; and then knocked my stupid head against something—the corner of that wardrobe, I suppose."

Newcomen looked at the sharply projecting upper corner of the wardrobe and found on it one small streak of blood.

"Are you badly done in?" he asked.

"No, my head's clearing. Even my forehead is padded with fat," answered Lucardo. "You see that to eat well and to drink well is a sort of life insurance."

"Someone was going through the old safe," said Newcomen. "Try to think again. I mean, the figure that slipped away through the door. Could that have been a woman, Lucardo?"

"Dinah," said Newcomen, "are you guilty?" She was
silent. "Answer me," he commanded.

"It could have been. Let me think. A woman or a man of not too many inches—yes, or even a tall man bent over as he ran. You see that it's no good. I can't give you a description."

"We have the job you interrupted, though," said Newcomen. "Can we make something out of that?"

They stood in front of the safe as Lucardo picked up the stack of papers, big and small, that had slipped out of the open door. Newcomen, on one knee, studied the array of old silver that filled the rest of the space inside the safe, objects which Dinah, it appeared, had not wished to be responsible for when she rented the house. He recognized some of the minor treasures of Thomas Decker, particularly four old silver goblets, hammered into exquisite form.

Lucardo was saying: "Drawings, *signore*. With the name of Dinah Moore on them."

Newcomen stood up suddenly and stared over the shoulder of Lucardo. The *marchese* was shuffling the stack of drawings slowly. A *podere* scene of olives and vines, Hans laughing at the world with a very villainous look, oxen swaying at the plow, and then scenes that had nothing to do with Italy, harbor bits, bridge building, a romantic English garden.

"What's it worth?" asked Newcomen.

"It's not worth a thief's time," said Lucardo.

"Are you sure?"

"I am sure. Good second-rate mechanics and some feeling, a good deal of feeling. But this cat in the sun is not feeling the heat of it, that hand on the scythe is holding no weight. Second rate, second rate. No Italian thief would steal this stuff."

"I thought she had a gift," said Newcomen slowly.

"She had a gift that Thomas Decker wanted," said Lucardo. "She had her beauty, *signore*."

The *marchese* stopped his talk, and his shuffling of the drawings at the same moment, staring at something he had found.

"But *this,*" he said softly, "is worth a thief's time!"

"What is it?" asked Newcomen.

But the *marchese* had slapped the drawings together and tucked them under his arm. His eyes shone like the eyes of a great cat.

"Later, my friend; later!" he said. "But the first thing is to get these—drawings—back to the villa before someone murders us here."

"Murder?" said Newcomen, peering at him. "On account of the drawings of Dinah Moore?"

"Murder," said Lucardo, "on account of what I hold under my arm!"

NEWCOMEN, AT his telephone, reached Nicholas Decker first. To him Newcomen said: "You've read about it in the paper, of course. About the coming of Professor Emile Cardeaux, I mean. I wondered if you'd like to be on hand when he arrives, and see what a great detective looks like? He'll be doing his stuff as soon as he sees the thread, I believe, and he might be able to tell us something important right away."

Decker said: "It's a late call, but I'll be there, Tony. This Cardeaux—I've been trying to find out about him, and nobody knows."

"He's one of those under-cover fellows," said Newcomen. "You never read about him in headlines—he leaves that for the heads of the police—but the devil will be to pay half an hour after he's had a look at that thread. I'm certain."

He got Nancy Ormonde.

"Of course I'd like to come," she said. "But all this about Professor Cardeaux—it doesn't really seem possible that he can read the mind of a bit of thread, do you think?"

"I'll tell you what," answered Newcomen. "It's said that he spotted one murderer through a pinch of dust that was shaken out of his pocket."

"Tony!" cried the girl.

"It's true, I believe," lied Newcomen.

"Then I'm going to come down and have a look at the monster," she declared.

He even rang Hugh Churchill at the hotel where the former secretary was staying for the night.

"You've seen a good deal of what's gone on, Churchill," said Newcomen. "Why not come up and see the great detective at work? You might even help him if he has questions to ask."

"Delighted," said Churchill. "Of course I'll be there. But isn't it a little odd to bring this French fellow down here when it's admitted that Lucardo is the killer?" He laughed a bit as he rang off.

Newcomen went up to his rooms and passed into the small inner chamber where Lucardo waited for him, stretched in a comfortable chair with his hands folded behind his head and only the twist of the handkerchief around his brow to disturb the perfect peace in his huge face. His eyes were closed, and they did not open when Newcomen came into the room.

"People will begin to drift in in about half an hour," said Newcomen. "We'll have everybody you suspect except Dinah Moore."

"How shall I see the party?" asked Lucardo.

"There are several flaws in the glazing of the studio window," said Newcomen. "From the outside you can look in as you please."

"That's a wet business," said Lucardo. "Do you think that anything really may come out of it?"

"I think something may," answered Newcomen. "Otherwise it makes a fool out of Cardeaux and out of me."

"This Cardeaux," said Lucardo softly, "it's strange that I haven't heard a word about him."

"He works quietly," said Newcomen.

"Ah, and that's true," answered Lucardo, "but I've spent my life listening to whispers. However," he went on, holding up his fat hand, "let's see what we shall have when everyone is assembled, even including Dinah Moore."

Newcomen wheeled on him.

"She won't be there," he declared. "She's not fool enough to walk back into trouble after what she's done tonight."

"You mean when she returned to the *villino?* You think that *she* really was the person I found at the safe in her room?" asked Lucardo.

"I think so," nodded Newcomen. "But she'll never appear here tonight."

"I have a hundred lire to say that she will," said Lucardo.

"I cover your hundred," answered Newcomen.

IT WAS toward eleven-thirty when Nancy Ormonde arrived at the villa and was shown into the studio. Nicholas Decker and Hugh Churchill already were there with Newcomen. She was wearing a dress of dead white with crystal buckles flaming at the insteps of her slippers. The slippers had red heels and there was a brilliant red lining to one fold of the dress hanging down from the shoulders behind. She had a yellow cloak, too, a pale Venetian thing covered with an arabesquing of embroidery, and she kept this on because the rain had blown a cold damp breath through the great room. A small fire burned on the hearth, but that was a mere handful of warmth in so large a chamber.

Nancy said to Newcomen: "But this is the very room, isn't it? Isn't this the very room where Tom was stabbed? They proved that, didn't they? I think poor Lucardo told me they had proved that."

"Yes, they proved that," said Newcomen.

"You look frightful, Tony," said the girl, still hardly more than whispering. "What have you been doing? Staying up all night and trying to catch the murderer with your *mind?*"

"I suppose the murderer is the *marchese,* after all," said Newcomen. "They're all after him."

"I don't know," said Nancy, searching his face. "I was fond of poor Lucardo, but you're what I worry about now. Tony, you mustn't do it! Sit down and talk to me for five minutes by the fire, won't you?"

"Why haven't I been seeing you?" asked Newcomen. "Tomorrow, you know what I'm going to do?"

"Something with me. Tony. That's what I hope, at least," she answered.

"I'm going to go up and sit on your terrace in the sun, if you'll be somewhere about in the garden. Picking at things. Giving the gardeners reprimands about something. It won't waken me if I can have the sun and the sound of your voice."

"You know, Tony, you ought not to talk like this," said Nancy Ormonde. "When you talk like this, a girl's imagination picks up what you say and runs on with it. For instance. I've been expecting you every day. But it was Dinah, wasn't it, who took up all your time?"

"Go on and talk, Nancy," he said. "I don't care what you say. But your voice runs through me like a river of peace. I mean to be poetic, just like that—a river of peace, a sweet, small river of peace."

"Well, it *was* Dinah, of course," she said. "That damn Dinah!" She laughed, and nodded at her idea. "She *is* so frightfully beautiful, Tony, isn't she? Don't say yes. Just be thoughtful and shrug your shoulders. That's better."

The butler came over and told him that someone wanted him in the outer room. He went into the big storage hall, and saw a woman hooded from head to foot in a dripping, shining black cape. She turned a little and he saw the face of Dinah.

"I thought you wouldn't show up," said Newcomen.

"Anthony," she said, "come back over here a little, so that people can't hear. Now, will you listen?"

"I've always listened to you," he said.

"Out there between the young cypresses and the wall, beside the studio window, there's a man standing in the rain," she said.

"Is there?" answered Newcomen. "I'll attend to that."

"You know that he's there?" she asked, searching his face to find something behind his words. "You know that it's Marchese Lucardo?"

"Well?" said Newcomen.

"You trust him, Anthony," breathed the girl, "but you mustn't. You think that he's a great-hearted man; but what you've discovered is just a brain. There's no real kindness in him. There's no real truth. He's a sham throughout. I tell you I know what he is. And it makes me shudder to think!"

"Of course it does," said Newcomen. "He's the man who murdered Thomas Decker and poor Bertelli, isn't he? Everybody knows that."

"Tony," she said, "for the sake of your own life…"

"You'd better come in and get warm by the fire," said Newcomen.

"I won't stay," she said.

"Yes, you'll stay," insisted Newcomen.

He pulled the wet of the cloak from about her. She was wearing the same travelling suit, with the white collar rumpled a bit with moisture.

"You came up here to watch over me, didn't you?" asked Newcomen. "That was sweet of you, dear."

"Anthony—there's murder in the air, in there. And Lucardo—"

"Be still about him, will you?" commanded Newcomen. "And do as you please. Come in or go away."

"I'll come in," said Dinah Moore.

"I thought you would," said Newcomen.

HUGH CHURCHILL called her attention as she went in. He kept his place near the desk of Thomas Decker. A small bottle such as aspirin is kept in, lay on the desk near the telephone.

Churchill was pointing it out to Nancy Ormonde.

"The thread inside is so small that you can barely make it out against the white of the label," said Churchill. "It's a small snake, but it's going to sting someone to death. Someone in this room, I wonder?"

Nicholas Decker had made himself at ease in one of the comfortable chairs. He was dressed in tails because he had just come from a dinner party, and the points of his collar pushed painfully up into his throat.

He said: "Is that where they found the blood. Churchill?"

"Yes. Just there," said Churchill, pointing. "Just a few drops. But that was enough to show that he had been stabbed in this room. And that changed everything. All the earlier theories went out like lights when the blood was discovered."

"Poor Tom falling in the midst of his career. You see the visible career all round you," said Nicholas Decker. He waved his hand. "Ten thousand bits of rather spoiled paintings and bric-a-brac. But does anybody put any faith in this miracle of the thread?"

"You'll see," said Churchill. "That thread is going to grow into the hangman's rope. It really is. And it will probably throttle somebody in this room."

"That's the second time you've said that," remarked Decker with irritation. "But what nonsense, Churchill. My good fellow, what rot!"

The thin face of Churchill twisted with a poison of malice.

"Do you think that Mr. Newcomen asked us here for nothing?" he demanded.

He pointed to the faces in the room one by one.

"Everybody here had a chance to commit the murder, and everybody had a motive!" he declared loudly.

Heads turned quickly.

No one spoke until Newcomen said: "Begin with me, Churchill, won't you? Point out my motives."

Churchill rubbed his hands together and shrugged his shoulders and laughed like a woman, with a high squeal of excitement in his voice.

"That would be ingratitude to my former employer," he said.

"Oh, carry on," said Newcomen. "Be Nemesis, Churchill. That's the sort of part you like."

"He looks more like a starved Adam than a Nemesis," said Nicholas Decker. "Adam with the apple stuck in his throat." No one laughed except Churchill, who was shuddering with nervous delight. He darted a finger at Newcomen, like a bird picking something out of the air.

"Motives and facts together," said Churchill. "Mr. Decker learns that Mr. Newcomen is returning to Italy in haste, and at once becomes very nervous. A doctor is called in. Sedatives. Brandies in the morning. When I speak of Mr. Newcomen's approaching arrival, he shuts me up with a rude word or two."

Churchill broke off to laugh and nod again, and again he made the darting gesture toward Newcomen.

"Mr. Newcomen reaches Italy and can't wait to reach Mr. Decker. He rushes by automobile from Venice at night and arrives in the dawn, at just about the hour when Mr. Decker died. Strange, isn't it? And as for motive, we know that Mr. Decker was mishandling the Newcomen millions. I handled some of the correspondence and I know."

IN THE pause Nancy Ormonde said: "I don't know why we should listen to this croaking."

"Ah, you know," said Nicholas Decker. "Skeleton at the feast. Let him rattle his bones a little."

"I killed Tom Decker?" asked Newcomen calmly. "But what about Bertelli, who seems to have been killed by the same hand?"

"Motives?" said Churchill. "Why, Bertelli had seen the first crime and was blackmailing you. How do we know it was blackmail? Because in what other way would he have got hold of the money with which he was paying his debts recently? Who would have trusted Bertelli with a loan? What other way did he have of raising money? No—blackmail, and then murder!"

"I don't know how the rest of you feel, but I simply won't listen to any more," said Nancy Ormonde. "Tony, what a patient dear you are!"

"The old hawk is free from the leash," said Nicholas, "and I like the way he stoops and kills for himself. See him shiver with pleasure, won't you? Eating malice like meat. And what about *me,* Churchill? Put your beak into me, won't you?"

Churchill giggled like an old maid.

"Of course you couldn't live except as your cousin helped you," said Churchill, "and people who take charity always hate the hand that feeds them. You hated Thomas Decker, he despised you, and finally there was the affair of the picture; he cut off your income, and I heard you threaten to take his life. I heard you, in the library, that morning when—"

"You contemptible..." Nicholas Decker roared. But he controlled himself and drew himself back into the chair with the strength of his arms against his legs, as it were. "The king's fool has to have license," he said, "though sometimes the dog must get a beating as well as a crust of bread."

Churchill went on: "Bertelli was your crony. He saw the crime. That's why you killed him afterward."

Nicholas Decker writhed in his chair, but he said: "Good! Very good! Logical, and all that. Now that we talk of suspects, what of our friend Churchill, here, who thinks his paintings are worth a fortune and who hated Tom because the big collector wouldn't boost him into some sales? Look at Churchill! A man made for hate. See it in his narrow face. The fool's gold that the devil put in his eyes to keep shining there. Notice that nobody had such excellent opportunities to kill his master. And, as he says, Bertelli saw the crime, and because of that he murdered Bertelli, too.

With a little feminine stiletto. Listen to his laugh. The scrawny animal! But he was mentioned pretty liberally in Tom's will, and of course if he killed his master before Tom had a chance to draw up a new document…"

"Steady," urged Newcomen. "Steady, please. This is getting a little out of hand."

"Shall I go on to the ladies, then?" asked Churchill, though he still stared at Nicholas Decker with venomous hunger.

"No, we've had enough," said Newcomen.

"Ah, but that's really not fair," said Nancy. "We're all buzzard's food, it seems. You don't mind, Dinah, do you, dear?"

CHURCHILL ACCEPTED this permission eagerly. He softened his voice, however, and made his manner more ingratiating.

"It's just the game, Miss Ormonde," he said, bowing over her, and vainly trying to rub warmth into his skinny hands. "In the game we try to make it as black as possible for everyone. But to take up your case, Miss Ormonde—you permit me?"

"Of course I permit you," said Nancy, sitting up a little straighter and looking at him with a bright interest.

"Well," said Churchill, "when one sees beauty, one thinks of childhood and innocence. Pretty, sweet things that can't do much wrong. Their hands are too small to do much wrong, one thinks. But after all, there is passion. Rare souls feel rare passions. Common people—we break bread; the rare souls break hearts and eat 'em. Pardon me, Miss Ormonde."

He bowed to her again and kept his head down a minute.

"Interesting," said Nicholas Decker, pointing his mustaches with his soft fingers. "See how the wolf puts his teeth even in that game! See him bow to cover his grin. The devil has laid a hand on you, Nancy. Aren't you shuddering?"

"Not a bit," she said, smiling on them all, and then looking back at Churchill.

"Motives—we come to motives," said Churchill. "And there is the will of Thomas Decker that makes Miss Ormonde quite rich. Oh, very well off, indeed. But suppose he should change that will? And was he about to change it? Was he about to turn away from beautiful Miss Ormonde to beautiful Miss Moore?"

Churchill stiffened and thrust out his arm at Nancy.

"You know he was!" he cried out suddenly. "You know he'd gone mad about Miss Moore! I've seen him sit hours in the chapel to watch her hands at work on the frescoes, like a child, watching; smiling like a child also. You knew he was going mad about her, and you stabbed him, and let him die. And Bertelli saw you, and that was why you were so much with him after the death of Thomas Decker, until he began to cost you too much money, and then you murdered Bertelli, too, with the same slender little bright knife that fits your hand so well...."

"Churchill!" called Newcomen.

The man stopped, panting; and the noise of every indrawn breath was as though he drank.

"But I don't mind, Tony; I really don't," said Nancy. "Foul things are bound to handle us, finally. Graves and worms and things. I don't mind. I only hope the poor monster will make a better Christian of me. Are *you* going to mind, Dinah?"

Dinah Moore looked not at Churchill but at Newcomen. "No," she said. "I won't mind." She looked at the wavering flame of the fire and shook her head, smiling a little. "No, I won't mind," she repeated.

"Well," said Churchill, settling gradually to a new theme from his last ecstasy, "we all see that Miss Ormonde is lovely; but Miss Moore is something still greater. People who have seen her once do not need pictures afterward. But motives—we come to motives—and there is the matter of the money which had to be sent away so constantly, and where would she get that money to send except from Thomas Decker? The money to send to America to—ah, well, the name doesn't matter, because he's not in the case, though he may be the cause behind everything. Money, then, from Thomas Decker, and how can she repay him? With herself? Given to an ageing, lecherous, evil man—ah, there would be strength in her hand to put an end to the bargain! If she wanted her path cleared, she would have the power to clear it. Do you doubt?"

She lifted her head and looked with unfathomable eyes at Newcomen, and he shuddered under the gaze.

"That's enough, Churchill," he said. "That's quite enough."

"A grim, graveyard effect, at that," said Nicholas Decker. "The man should have been a preacher, or a seller of pardons. But when does the great detective arrive, Tony? When are we to watch him peer at the thread in the bottle and point a finger at one of us?"

He leaned over the desk and cried out: "But hold on! There's no thread in the bottle at all!"

"I thought so," cried Newcomen. "I thought it would be changed. Stand fast everyone and don't move. Keep in your places. I thought the sham might do well enough. Churchill was right. We've got a murderer here among us. In the room. One of you that I'm watching. No great detective is coming. His name was only a bait to draw you. And one poor, guilty devil has taken the hook. He's changed the phial for an empty bottle. The one that the other bottle is found on is the certain killer."

"Very melodramatic," said Nicholas Decker. "I suppose we can sit down again, at least? Will there have to be a search, and all that?"

He followed his own suggestion by dropping back into the deep chair which he had been in before. Some of the others were moving when a great blow smashed in the whole lower section of the studio window. The glass fell with a long uproar across the floor, and through the gap the voice of Lucardo shouted: "Dinah Moore—stand off by yourself!"

DINAH MOORE had been slipping down onto the couch beside Nancy Ormonde, but that sudden thunder with her name in it made her spring up again.

Lucardo, stepping through the huge, broken archway of the window onto the floor of the studio, called again: "Stand away there against the wall, *signorina*. And all the rest keep your places. Watch them, Newcomen. A bit of sleight of hand still can spoil everything."

Nicholas Decker, taking his ease, lifting his chin to clear the jowls from the collar wings, observed: "Well, Franco, I never expected to see you again except in jail; but now I see that you've arranged a little farce with Tony, and I hope I'm going to enjoy it. But what if the police arrive in time to interrupt the show?"

"Sit quietly and be at peace, my friend," said Lucardo. "The police will come when they are called, but first we want a stillness about us, since quiet is a first necessity for thought."

He picked up a straight chair and placed it against the wall.

"Sit down, Miss Moore," he requested.

She obeyed him.

Nancy Ormonde said, audibly: "Poor Dinah! Could you have guessed it? Could you really have imagined such a thing?"

Lucardo threw back his cloak and tossed it onto a chair, revealing a thick package under the pit of his left arm. He was saying: "Well done, Newcomen! After all, we humans turn out to be simple people; and a new device from a New World is enough, it seems, to charm the birds out of the trees. Mr. Churchill, will you remain in the room?"

Churchill had been edging toward the door. He cried out something over his shoulder about a "free man" and made a sudden break for liberty. If the door had been open he would have got through it, but the necessary instant of delay enabled Newcomen to reach him. He wilted down almost to his knees under the grasp of the big man and clawed at the hand of Newcomen, whining:

"What have I done? What do you want with me? I've only told a little truth, and it is the truth!"

"Stand up and be yourself," advised Newcomen grimly. "No one is going to break you up. Take that chair and be still in it."

Churchill sank into the chair. The fear in his eyes ranged shamelessly around the group, hunting for an explanation which he could not find.

The *marchese,* during this moment of bustling interruption, remained perfectly still, but with a glance that included everyone in the room. Now he began to unwrap the parcel he was holding.

"If I can have your attention," he said, "we'll leave the matter of the thread and the bottle, the very beautiful device of my friend Newcomen. We can return to that later. For the moment I'd like to talk to you about another matter." But here the butler came in and peered for a moment at the odd immobility of that group of guests, and above all at the commanding figure of the fat *marchese* who stood in the centre of the floor.

"What is it?" asked Newcomen. "Yes, you're seeing Marchese Lucardo. When you have a moment you can telephone for the police, if you please. I think we'll be ready for them when they arrive. But what brought you into the room?"

"It's Beppo, *signore,*" said the butler. "He has just learned that *Signorina* Moore is here in the house and he begs you to see him for a moment."

"I can't see him," snapped Newcomen.

"*Signore,* it is a matter of life and death," said the butler. "It is a matter of your own safety!"

"Let Beppo come in," said Lucardo. "We must have time for our friends. The rest of you, please observe that I am watching you with great care. When you move your hands, move them openly, if you please, so that they may be seen every instant."

BEPPO CAME in with his hat in his hands.

"Now, Beppo?" asked Newcomen.

Beppo showed a twist of paper.

"*Signore,*" he said, "for a long time I have kept an eye on the *villino,* hoping to keep away the evil in it, and the day before yesterday I saw the *signorina* leaving. The automobile came as far as the entrance and there it stopped. I saw the *signorina* lean out and drop what looked like a shower of small green leaves on the ground; and while she dropped them, she was looking back toward the house. *Signore,* I am an old man and age has not made me altogether foolish. I have seen charms made, in my time, and I have seen whole families ruined by cruel witches."

He drove the gesture which defies the evil eve straight at Dinah Moore as he spoke.

"Go on quickly, Beppo," said Newcomen, frowning at the old gardener.

"As soon as the car drove on," said Beppo, "I hurried to see what sort of herbs she had dropped on the good honest ground of my *signore.* But what I found was not leaves but little bits of green paper."

He held up the twist with his right hand, being careful to keep the paper far from his face as he did so.

"There was no wind, *signore,*" he went on, "and I picked up the bits of paper, every one. Afterward I brought them home and showed them to Angelina. We began to move the pieces of paper around on the table, and at last, this afternoon, Angelina saw a terrible thing. She saw your name appear, *signore,* when certain of the scraps of paper were put together!"

Beppo stopped, panting fast with his excitement.

He said: "Then we moved the pieces of paper this way and that until another great miracle appeared: The name of *Signorina* Moore! I knew then, that it was a terrible spell, and I came running back to the house, so that you could burn the thing and pray for your soul while the smoke went up toward the sky. But when I came to the house, I heard that the *signorina* herself was here. So I ran here fast, fast—sainted heavens how my knees still tremble!—so that you could make her face her work. There, *signore!* It is there!"

He held out the twist of paper, and Newcomen took it with a grave face.

"I think you've done a great thing for me," he said. "Now go back to bed, Beppo. Tomorrow morning I'll show you that I know the people who love me. Good night."

"Happy night!" said the old Tuscan. "Happy night, *signori!*"

"Dinah, is it the cheque?" asked Newcomen, as Beppo disappeared through the door.

She looked at him with eyes too abstracted to understand what he said. He opened the twist of paper and poured the small heap of fragments into the palm of his hand. It was not hard to recognize in a moment the sign of twenty-five hundred dollars which he had scratched on the money line of the cheque. He replaced the bits of paper in the twist and dropped it into his pocket.

Lucardo had finished unwrapping his parcel and held it up now in both hands.

"All my dear friends," he said, "we have worked out a case in the murder of Thomas Decker in this room. We have worked out all except one strange point. We come to that now. I hold in my hands some drawings by Miss Moore, who had locked them in her safe. Will you tell me why they were locked in the safe, Miss Moore?"

"I'd never paid much attention to them," said Dinah Moore. "But a short time ago I began to think they might have a value after all. So I put them in the old house safe."

"What made you put them in the safe?"

"Well, I had a talk with Miss Ormonde. She seemed to think they had a value."

"They have, you know," said Nancy Ormonde. "They're really charming."

Beppo drove his gesture straight
at Dinah Moore. "I have seen
whole families ruined by
cruel witches," he said.

"I know about the visit you paid Miss Moore in the middle of the night," said Lucardo. "Insomnia sent you out for a drive. It was the day Thomas Decker died, wasn't it?"

"Yes, that night," nodded Nancy Ormonde. "I drove clear across town, and when I passed the *villino* and saw a light I just wondered if Dinah might be awake."

"I was reading," said Dinah.

"Will you tell us what happened?" asked Lucardo.

"While I was reading," said the girl, "Hans began to growl near the window. I went out on the balcony and saw someone move in the brush near the drive. I called out to ask who it was, and after a moment Nancy Ormonde came out into the open. She called and waved back to me. She said, 'I was just driving by and I thought that I'd call on you, Dinah. But then I thought that it was too late. It *is* too late, isn't it?' I told her to come in and she came."

"Did it seem strange to you, that visit?" asked Lucardo.

"Yes. It seemed a little strange. We'd never been very friendly."

"What was the talk about?"

"Well, she said that she'd never seen much of my work and she wondered if I would let her look at some of it."

"Did that seem an honest interest to you?" asked Lucardo.

"I wondered about it a little."

"And then you showed her some of your drawings?"

"Yes. I told her that most of them were quite worthless, I was afraid. Except to me as a sort of autobiography—of failure, in fact. But she seemed to like them. After she had looked at the drawings she advised me to put them away in a safe place. She said she thought she knew of a party who might be interested in buying them."

"So then you put them away in the safe?"

"Yes."

Lucardo turned to Nancy Ormonde.

"By the way," he said, "I've been in your house and I'd say you were a very good judge of values in drawings and paintings. Even *Signor* Decker asked your advice. Are these drawings quite fine, really?"

"Interesting. Very interesting," said Nancy earnestly. "They reveal so much—character, you know."

Lucardo took from the stack of drawings a typewritten sheet of paper.

"After all," he said, "that pile of drawings was worth a price. Because inside of it was the last will and testament of Thomas Decker, dated the last day of his life, witnessed by Nancy Ormonde and Bertelli. Do you remember witnessing it, Miss Ormonde?"

"No... Wait a moment... I do remember signing something for Tom. I didn't read it, I just signed," said Nancy Ormonde.

"You should have read it," said Lucardo.

"A new will? A brand-new will, really?" broke out Nicholas Decker. "Thank heaven for that! He must have given me a little more attention than in the other one. What did he give me, Franco?"

"To my dearly beloved cousin, Nicholas Decker," read the *marchese*, "I freely give and bequeath the good advice I already have given him."

"Ah!" murmured Decker. "Think of that, will you? Rather good, eh? Old Tom knew how to put the shot between wind and water, didn't he?"

He kept on smiling and polishing his mustaches, but his face was white.

CHURCHILL SEEMED to be half dazed during the last moments, but he managed to cry out now: "And me? And me?"

Lucardo made a half turn and read to him with unction: "To my devoted secretary, in token of his many years of busy service, I leave my wholehearted appreciation of him as he truly is."

Churchill could not quite understand this. He kept dodging a hand back and forth close to his chin as though the blow had not yet fallen. At last he said: "And Nancy Ormonde?"

"To my dear friend and cheerful companion, Nancy Ormonde," read Lucardo, "I leave that finer appreciation of fine things which we have worked out together."

"Is that all? Ha! Ha! Ha!" shouted Churchill, hysterical with happiness, and pointed at the girl a long skinny arm that jerked with his explosions of mirth.

Nancy Ormonde, turning to Dinah Moore, looking carefully at her, said: "And to Dinah? Something to Dinah, I dare say?"

"To Dinah Moore," read Lucardo, "I leave the *villino,* its furnishings, the outbuildings, and all the land attached to them, together with the income from my holdings in the Texwright Corporation to maintain the place properly."

"To me?" cried Dinah Moore. "To me?"

"And the rest of the property, as formerly, goes to Anthony Newcomen," concluded Lucardo. "Under the signatures there is a large blot which appears to be blood. I suppose analysis will tell whether or not it is the type of Tom Decker's blood. But I presume it was picked up in this room after the stabbing of Decker, That will make it a little more authentic."

"I'm rather overcome," said Nancy Ormonde, rising. "I didn't know poor Tom had such a vicious streak in him."

"Stay where you are, please," said Lucardo. "Newcomen, stop her!"

"You won't mind, Nancy—just another moment?" said Newcomen, meeting her with his outstretched hand.

She took his hand with both of hers.

"Please, Tony, dear!" she said, and smiled up at him.

"It's in the cloak, I suppose," said Lucardo, and gave the embroidered yellow cloak of Nancy a sudden shake. Something flashed down from it and rattled on the floor, spinning around and around as though it had the life of a wound-up toy. As it settled, those staring eyes in the room saw that it was another little aspirin phial exactly like the one which lay on the desk.

But more than that, they saw the sound of that fall strike suddenly through the body of the girl; her smile, also, froze and then broke as though her face were white fresh clay which the sculptor's hand had smeared across with inspired ugliness.

"The truth being, of course," said Lucardo, "that when Nancy Ormonde looked at your drawings that night, Dinah Moore, she hid this will among them. What damning evidence of motive for murder was locked up in your safe all that time! If you had been arrested because of the tassel and the stiletto, if the will had then been found, wouldn't we have wondered why you kept it locked in the safe instead of using it to claim your legacy? Would we have assumed that you were afraid to produce that will? Your conscience... And then with Bertelli and Miss Ormonde ready to deny their signatures as witnesses... Ah, Nancy, what a pity you didn't burn the thing, as you first intended! But as it is, Newcomen's bit of thread has tied itself around your throat. There is only one sort of aspirin sold in bottles here. You did not think you were running a great risk when you brought an empty bottle with you tonight—it would almost surely to identical with the bottle that held the thread. And it was!"

She threw back her head, but with her hands still pressed to her face, saying: "Take me away! I don't care. I'll tell whatever you want. But she's won—she's beaten me again—and don't make me see her. Don't let me see her face!"

"When you went to her house that night, it was to throw the stiletto into the garden of the *villino*—was that it?" asked Newcomen.

"Yes!" whispered Nancy. "If only I had thrown it into her heart!"

THE POLICE came and took Nancy Ormonde away with them so

quietly that Newcomen was not aware that she had gone, for he was saying to Dinah Moore: "If ever I suspect you again, darling—"

"Ah, but you will!" said Dinah Moore seriously.

"Never!" said Newcomen. "But all these days the thing that was a knife twisting in my heart was the thought of that fellow in America for whom you wanted the money."

"But his name was there in the desk when you searched it!" cried Dinah. "He's my brother, Anthony. Did you think...?"

"Ah!" breathed Newcomen, and closed his eyes and put back his head.

"Sit down!" said Dinah Moore.

Newcomen sat down.

"But you tore up the cheque," he said, still with his eyes closed while the old idea melted away forever from his mind. "And so how did you have money for the train? Or did you take the train at all?"

"Hush," said Dinah. "It doesn't matter. Keep your eyes closed. You're going to rest."

"I'm going to rest. Yes. But tell me. Let me have an armful of you and then tell me—now."

"There was one drawing in particular that Nancy said might be— valuable. I brought it up to her house. She had a queer, hungry look when she saw it. Rather a frightened look, too. I offered her the drawing for a hundred lire. It was enough to get me into the mountains."

"You were going there, Dinah? In spite of the brute way I'd treated you? You were going there to wait for me?"

"I was going there," said Dinah Moore.

"I don't dare open my eyes and look at you."

"Hush!" said the girl. "I went almost all the way, and then I noticed that the key to the house safe of the *villino* was gone from my purse. I thought back and knew that I couldn't have lost it except at Nancy's villa, where I'd left the purse behind me when I went into the bathroom. I knew then that she had it; and I guessed that there was something more than the drawings in her mind. I rushed back to Florence. I was glad of an excuse to come because I was afraid for you, Anthony. And the missing of the key decided me, I came back..."

"And we found you in the dark of that room. Dinah, how the sight of you went through me!"

"Be quiet, my dear."

"I *am* quiet. I'll always be quiet."

"I had such a dread of what might happen to you," she said, "that I even suspected Marchese Lucardo. But that's ended. It's all ended. The trouble's all gone."

"It's not all ended," said Newcomen. "You're going to lift me up out of this degradation and shame, aren't you, Dinah? You're going to marry me, aren't you?"

She began to laugh softly.

"Does it mean yes?" asked Newcomen. "Tell me what it means before I open my eyes, because I'm seeing a bigger dazzle and brightness than the whole Milky Way. Stars at noon? Why, Dinah, I'm seeing them with my eyes shut. Tell me if that's love or just nonsense."

"Just nonsense," said Dinah.

ON THAT shoulder of the hill—there, you see, where it slopes out?" said Lucardo.

"I see, *marchese,*" said the commissary of police.

"Right there the workmen start tomorrow, excavating. It will make a handsome terrace, eh?"

"It will, *signore,*" said the commissary, bowing.

"And in the middle of it there will be the swimming pool. Other minds than mine have insisted on that, because they know that a fat fish like a Lucardo loves to cool itself in the blue of water on a summer's day."

"Naturally," yawned the commissary, "but to return to the Decker-Bertelli affair, it is to assure you that I, *marchese,* never doubted for an instant, never for a moment questioned your innocence."

"What a friend you are," said Lucardo, yawning in his turn.

"But what in the first place put you on the proper track?" asked the commissary.

"It was the dagger, my friend. The delicate, fine-pointed knife that made me think of a woman's delicate, fine-drawn wit which penetrates through masculine absurdities with such ease, with so little effort, and pricks the bubbles of our ideas. So I thought of a woman's hand wielding the knife. I noted a very small thing, but an important one. A man using such a knife would have managed it with thumb and forefingers, like a hypodermic syringe. But in each case in the case of Bertelli, in the case of Decker the outer incision was not a mere puncture capable of admitting the blade. It was a slight cut. And that told me it had been grasped by the whole hand, with a downward stroke. A whole hand. A hand as small as a child's. Did you ever see the hand of Nancy Ormonde? So lovely! So like a child's. Hardly more mature. Soft. Dimpled across the knuckles. A hand to kiss and adore above all others..."

"Yes, yes!" said the commissary.

"There had been the strange happenings at the *villino,* of course. That matter of the poisoning, and Roberto. Someone hated Dinah Moore. Who? I thought at once of that exquisitely lovely, that fair and graceful girl, that Nancy Ormonde. The thought met me like a kiss upon the forehead, a signature, a promise of truth, and I felt that I was right."

"She stabbed Decker," said the commissary, looking into his notebook. "We have drawn most of it out of her. She stabbed Decker while he was at the telephone, telling *Signor* Newcomen in Venice the name of the person he feared. That name? It was her own, of course. For she had let him see the fury in her that same day. Think of the beast in the man! He was finished with her. Mind you, she had come here expecting to marry him and his money, but the other girl had rubbed her out of his mind. So he gives her on this day a paper to sign, and she does so, and afterward he reads her the paper, which is a new will, rubbing out her future. That was when the devil came up like a cat in her face, I suppose, and grinned at Decker.

"The shock of it made him call for a doctor. It made him telephone the only man he really could trust, also. So she slips back into the villa that evening and waits for him in the big study, and when he comes and sits at the telephone, she stabs him. She sees him fall on his face. In his fall, he paws from the top of the table the new will which lies there. She picks it up. When it is destroyed, the old will stands, and her fortune with it. It is a good stroke that she has made! She turns and with the axe which lies at hand, she cuts the telephone line—weak clumsy strokes, but the work soon is done. She turns from it to see a ghost. Her heart freezes. For there is Thomas Decker rising from the floor and walking toward the door. We have all that from her, *signor marchese.* Now tell me what happened, exactly, because you are sure to know."

"How should I know so surely?" asked the *marchese,* smiling.

"Because of the sympathy that is in you," said the commissary, covering the shudder of his body with a slight bow; "the sympathy which leads you straight into human minds and souls."

"I think, often, of the two servants in the outer hall," said Lucardo. "Do you remember how they described him? As though he were bent on a purpose, suddenly... Yes, he only knew one thing, not his pain, but his desire to get air, more air. And one said he looked like a man going to collect his rents, whereas we know that he was going to pay all his own arrears!"

Lucardo laughed pleasantly.

"Then into the garden, and one of them following him—that good Emilio who has been so useful to me while he was in jail!

Think of the dying man by the pool of the water lilies, and the murderer standing ready to murder a dead man—in the rain! Then the dying man falls and later he dies. And our sweet girl, our Nancy? She has slipped out of the place now, and down through the garden. Mind you, to kill Thomas Decker was only a small part of her purpose. To destroy the girl who had destroyed her chances—that was her first desire throughout."

"So she enters the *villino* garden to drop the stiletto in a safe place," said the commissary.

"A place where it might be found, as evidence against Dinah Moore."

"But she has not destroyed the will!" exclaimed the commissary. "That puzzles me. If you or I were a murderer—in our hands the bit of paper depriving us of a legacy—"

"Her first impulse, doubtless, was to destroy the will. Then, after she had cut the telephone wire, she saw Decker rise to his feet and go from the room. Has she failed, then? Will he live after all? What thoughts passed through her mind then? The will is in her hands, to destroy if she wishes. But she does not destroy it."

"But why? It is the one feature I do not understand."

"She is a clever woman, you understand. Where a stupid woman would destroy the will, Nancy Ormonde thinks ahead. Even more than the money, she desires the destruction of Dinah Moore. She may need that will some day. In her own country it is the law that a murderer—or murderess—cannot profit by the victim's will, if proved guilty of the crime. If Dinah Moore should be convicted of Decker's murder, then even if the will is discovered Dinah Moore will not benefit by it. So she thinks. In any case, how easy to break the will, to brand it a forgery, to deny her signature as witness, to persuade Bertelli to do likewise, and make the first will valid. Then the second will becomes merely a damning piece of evidence against Dinah Moore, the more damning if Dinah Moore does not produce it immediately after Decker's death.

"Dinah, I'm seeing stars at noon with my eyes shut. Tell me if that's love or just nonsense."

Even when I found that will among the drawings in the safe, I wondered—I wondered if Dinah Moore knew it was there and had been afraid to produce it, knowing she was under suspicion."

"Ah!"

"So this is what Nancy Ormonde will do. She will place the stiletto as evidence in Dinah Moore's garden—in a place where it will be found. The will, too, she will leave there. But hidden. If by some unlucky chance she has left a forgotten clue that may cause her to be suspected of the murder herself, then she will see to it that the will is conveniently discovered. It will save her and destroy Dinah Moore. If the evidence of the stiletto alone is sufficient to destroy Dinah Moore, then the will is to remain hidden. If more evidence is needed, Nancy Ormonde knows where it can be found."

The commissary rubbed his hands. "Indeed, yes, she thought ahead. Far ahead."

"She enters the *villino* garden. No human eye can detect her, but the nose and eyes of a beast may. And it is a beast who sees the human beast at work and calls the mistress from her bed. Before Nancy Ormonde can place the stiletto and bury the will, the dog scents her. She flings the stiletto away—and later it is the dog that finds the weapon and hides it in the grotto. Nancy Ormonde, still with the will in her purse, is forced to make some excuse to explain her presence to Dinah Moore."

"I see, I see," said the commissary, nodding vigorously.

"So in a few moments we have them smiling and talking together. Both so fresh and young, and one of them strong because she has been feeding on death like a bee on a delicious flower. Nancy Ormonde thinks of the drawings. As she looks at them her mind is at work. Dinah Moore seldom looks at the drawings any more. Nancy Ormonde slips the will among them and advises Dinah Moore to lock the drawings in the safe. She may find a market for them. She may be back. The will, giving Dinah Moore part of the estate of a murdered man, is locked safely in Dinah Moore's safe, and the stiletto that let the life out of Decker's body is lying in Dinah Moore's garden. More than that, when Nancy talked with Dinah that night, Dinah was wearing a green dressing gown and on the table was a green tassel that had become frayed and that had broken from the cord. A use for it entered Nancy's mind and she slipped it into her purse. So Nancy goes home, but a devil is treading on her heels."

"Bertelli?" queried the commissary.

"Like a true Italian, he cannot bear it that such a flower of a girl should be wasted entirely on such a withering fellow as Decker. He has been trying to fill up some odd moments of Nancy's time. He has been haunting her, and this night he has haunted her all the way to the Decker villa. Through the studio window, he has seen the blow struck."

"He saw the murder!"

UNDOUBTEDLY. HE has followed her again through the garden to the *villino*. But when she comes out to her car, which stands a little down the road, he accosts her, rides part of the way home with her. Love? No, he is not such a fool as to talk about love when there is money to be had. She has plenty of money; he has none. He has, however, knowledge. Will she pay? Yes, she will pay! But when Bertelli accosts her like a polite devil, and she realizes that they must now be allies, she makes him prove his courage and usefulness at once by taking the little tassel back to the house and throwing it into the empty study."

"And there Newcomen finds it," said the commissary.

"It is in his pocket next morning when he goes down to see Dinah Moore. Why has he gone down? Because when he arrived that morning, on a naked spot on the lawn he has seen the print of the foot of a dog in the mud, a dog lacking a toe in a front foot. And he has learned that such a dog belongs in the *villino*. Notice him, then, on the trail of murder with one clue in his pocket. And when he sees Dinah Moore, she is wearing the green dressing gown with one tassel gone from it.

"Shall he turn Dinah over to the police at once? He should, of course. But a breath of love has entered him. To the boy, it is a torment of exquisite pain. He will not turn her over to the police. He will devour her time. He will have her entirely to himself for a mystic period of seven days—it might as well have been three or nine, the romance would have been the same. But he buys her time; he enslaves her for a week; and that is the week of his joy and misery."

"And in the meantime," said the commissary, "Nancy Ormonde—"

"A prize a thousand times greater than Decker has crossed her horizon. Newcomen, young, brave, intelligent, enormously wealthy. But no sooner does she open fire on him than she discovers that he is spending his time with Dinah. It maddens her. Always Dinah in the path. And now she knows fear. The green tassel has not been found—not by the police at any rate. The stiletto has not been found. There is no case against Dinah Moore, and now she realizes that if the will should be discovered her own claim on the Decker estate will be wiped out, with not even revenge to pay her for the loss. For Bertelli has told her something. The law in Italy is not the same as in her native State—even a murderer may benefit by the will of his victim in Italy. The crime does not affect the will.

"Bertelli is frightened when he hears about the will. In hiding it among Dinah's drawings she was not clever, he declares, but guilty of sheer folly. On his own account, he is afraid. He would lose his own legacy. As to denying his signature as witness to the new will and contesting it if it is discovered—well, Bertelli sees risk and trouble in that. Much simpler to get the will back and destroy it.

"He makes one attempt to get his hands on the drawings, but he is interrupted by Newcomen. The drawings, he knows, are kept locked in the safe."

The commissary interrupted: "But why did Nancy Ormonde not ask to see the drawings again? She had already pretended an interest in buying them?"

"After Bertelli's failure—and he must have made the attempt on his own account—Nancy Ormonde was afraid to show any further interest in the drawings. Newcomen had thrown Bertelli out of the house. Perhaps he had become suspicious, examined the drawings, found the will. Nancy now wishes she had not been so very clever, that she had not looked so far ahead. She wants that will."

Lucardo gazed dreamily out over the hillside. The commissary waited.

"At any rate, the thing now is to get the key to the safe. Bertelli cannot do it. But there is that dishonest Roberto who was discharged by Nancy for theft, when she could have jailed him as well. Yes, there is that Roberto, who can be further corrupted with a handsome present and a promise of more. So the poisoned fish appears on the table. But, again, there is Newcomen like a guardian devil to spoil all plans. This Newcomen is becoming too dangerous, in fact. He is prying too closely into matters. He even seems to be suspecting delicate Nancy herself. Therefore he must go down! He has pointed a finger of suspicion at Bertelli, above all!

"So they plan the thing together, she and Bertelli. He waits in an appointed place in a dark alley. The girl leads the victim through... But on the way Newcomen gives way to nature enough to make love to her a little. For how can young people be long together without a bit of love to sustain them? And as he speaks, she wonders with a desperate sudden hope whether she may not be able to snare this golden fish out of the blue pool of heaven? Millions, millions of dollars, not lire! She changes her mind at the last instant. She sees the gun at the window and springs in between... Oh, that was gallant, brave Nancy! But still the American is not in your hand! Dinah, like a witch, still holds him."

LUCARDO CONTINUED: "Bertelli, however, is not a fool. He is made to think twice when the girl changes her mind in the alley. If she changes her mind once, she may again. Besides, she is death. He knows that. He has seen her act. Therefore he determines to do something of his own accord. He telephones to Newcomen and bargains with him to sell the name of the murderer of Thomas Decker, and Newcomen closes with the offer, though it is high. They are to meet in my house, because Bertelli seeks the crowd to cover him. He would not have Nancy suspect him. Not while she is still a free agent. Nevertheless she distrusts him, she *does* see him talking with Newcomen, and she knows that something must be done at once. What man could have moved through all the possibilities so quickly and arrived at the right answer so surely? In a moment she is at the telephone; a moment later the call comes through for Bertelli, and he is taken away from Newcomen at the very moment when he is about to give the name of the murderess. She waits for him behind the office door. For two days, so great is her distrust of Bertelli, she has carried a stiletto. As he sits down to the phone, she stabs him from behind as she had stabbed Decker."

Lucardo sighed.

"And so to the end, with poor Lucardo hunted like a rabbit through the fields and not able to stand and protest his innocence because he must not waste time fighting the law while this case is growing to a head. At last Nancy has her chance to reach for the will. Dinah has come to her; Dinah has given her the opportunity to steal the key; and Dinah's house is empty. So Nancy comes in the night."

"And finds you there, *signor marchese*," said the commissary, with his ready bow. "Ah, that was brilliant deduction, my friend."

"Deduction?" sighed Lucardo. "Shall I tell you the truth? It was only that I knew many strange events had happened in the *villino*. I went there mysteriously, with Newcomen half expecting someone might be in it, because so many attempts had been made on Dinah, or on something in her possession. Now that she was gone, I argued, the blow might fall there, and I wanted to be present. That was the only reason. That was why we interrupted our bright Nancy when she was at the safe. And so the end came with Newcomen's bit of thread in a bottle strangling our lady in the end."

"And that was Newcomen's idea?" said the commissary, curiously.

"Absolutely his. An exquisite idea of bluff. How could I have thought of it?"

"We must assign credit," said the commissary. He shifted a little from his place. "We *must* assign credit for this brilliant work, my friend."

"To *Signor* Newcomen you can assign nothing," said Lucardo. "He will not have his name mentioned. He has found happiness for himself, and he does not wish to be mentioned as bringing unhappiness to others. And as for me... I think more of the new swimming pool than of crime, just now. Besides, was not all the work done in your department, my dear friend?"

"Ah, that is true," said the commissary, breathing a long sigh and settling back in his place. "After all, it is department work, even though our great Lucardo is a part of it."

"But only a part," said Lucardo.

"True, only a part," said the commissary.

"Without you, what could I do? Without the thousand possibilities you pour into my hands, the courtesies of the entire *gendarmerie,* the efficiency of your secretaries, your own wise advice..."

"*Signor marchese,* you overwhelm me!"

"My dear friend, I speak only the truth."

"You will dine with me soon, *marchese?*"

"Whenever it is your pleasure."

"As for the newspapers, I must throw them a few bones. For yourself, you are sure you do not care?"

"Nothing whatever."

"Well, a great spirit like yours, *signor marchese,* cannot be fed on newsprint... The swimming pool and the new terrace," he added, rising, "will improve everything in the valley. They will pour on you the sort of happiness you deserve... I see a tall man and a woman coming up from the lower *podere*. Are they friends?"

"That pair?" said Lucardo. "Ah, they are two children who have adopted me. That is all."

Devil Dog

SAMUEL CORNWALL GRESHAM was one of those fellows who have the blunt, square jaw of a fighter, and the will power to hold on. As a matter of fact he had a lot of fighting to do, because his habit was not to take advice but to figure out everything for himself. For instance, when he wanted to go through a medical school he decided to make the money for it by digging gold. The place in which he chose to dig gold was Alaska; the particular spot he selected was one of those dreary little forests scattered through a bog frozen over in winter; and the methods he chose were what he found written up in books about '96.

No one but a convinced old sourdough or a Samuel Cornwall Gresham would have faced the loneliness of that existence single-handed, but it never occurred to Gresham to look for a partner. He wanted to dig his own money and save it, by himself. He never had asked another human being into his life. He had no friends. He never had been in love, and one look at his grim face, always set toward tomorrow's purpose, was enough to freeze up all the joy and fun and affection in any girl.

His purpose now was to save $1,600. A four-year medical course, eight months a year, $50 a month, would cost $1,600. In his first Alaskan year he travelled as a stowaway and work-away, then did manual labor at the high Alaskan rates, got together some dogs, discovered that the biggest of the lot was only a six-months-old puppy which he therefore sold, and finally followed a foolish barroom story to the district in which he pegged out his claim. Then, through the dark of the winter, he cut frozen trees to make fires to thaw the frozen ground of the bog, and labored and mucked and washed until he had $500 out of the soil, at the $35 rate.

This second winter found him at the same toil, a brutal, grinding, blind life. In it he kept no count of days. There was no clock in his existence except the annual set of the sun, the rising of it, the thaw and freezing of the great river. When he had worked to exhaustion, he turned into his sleeping bag; when the walls of his stomach clove together with starvation, he warmed frozen beans in a frying pan together with pork grease, and ate. He lived with his face turned to the ground. Even the aurora borealis could not draw up his soul and his eyes to thank God for the beauty of the "merry dancers." He merely found the light a winter convenience; and as the months went by one deep, black wrinkle was carved deeper and deeper between his eyes.

When he roused from sleep, his body begged pitifully for more repose, on this day of the second winter, but as usual he took two or three deep breaths while he summoned that resolution which used his body as a wretched slave; then he got up, started the fire in the stove which was his chief treasure, and put on the pan of beans; they rattled like marbles into the skillet. His two dogs sat down and watched him with starving eyes. He put two small frozen fish, which he had brought from the shed, into a pot with some snow. When they were thawed, he gave a fish to each dog.

The stove turned red-hot. Above the level of its top the air in the little log cabin was almost tropically warm, but his legs walked around in hoarfrost. There had been a big change in temperature. He could hear the frost gnawing its teeth deeper into the trees outside.

That was when the door opened and Jarvis stood on the threshold with a rifle. He knew Jarvis because it was to him that he had sold the overgrown puppy a year and a half before. Jarvis was as big as a mountain but he was a beast, not a man. Instead of a beard he had fur on his face, and his breath had sheathed the hair on his chin with ice. Gresham's two dogs, Midge and Charley, knew that it was not a man but a brute. They came out of their corner with the devil in their eyes and their teeth bared, snarling.

Jarvis said: "Chris, take 'em!"

The biggest thing that Gresham ever had seen in the way of a dog or a wolf slid in past his master. He was covered with a soft grey fluff against the Arctic weather.

He had a white vest and a white mark of wisdom between his eyes.

Then he "took" those two big huskies as a timber wolf would take a pair of lap dogs. Two or three slashes, like sword strokes laid Charley dead; Midge, horribly wounded, screamed like a woman and died in turn.

Jarvis kicked the door shut. He kept his rifle pointing at Gresham all the time.

"What d'you want?" asked Gresham.

"Chuck," said Jarvis. "Where's it kept?"

"In the shed," said Gresham. He was about to say that he had just enough to last him through the winter, but then he realized that a thing which began with dog-murder would not be settled by any vocal appeal.

Jarvis pointed Gresham out to the great dog and said: "Maybe you know him well enough to understand that he's gotta be watched, so—watch!"

Then he turned his back, kicked open the door of the shed, and carried the lantern into the dark of it. There was only a vague light left behind. It came from the red of the stove sides, and from the cracks of the stove door, besides the shifts and wanderings of pale lantern light as Jarvis moved about in the shed. There was not much need of light, however, for Gresham was not tempted to try to escape; he could see too much of Chris by the wild green devil in the eyes of that dog. The husky, or overgrown wolf, or whatever he was, was like a whole tornado ready to go and only restrained by a silken little spiderthread of uncertainty. He seemed to be reaching slowly for the kill as he stuck out his blood-stained muzzle by degrees, with his mane ruffed up and his lip curled back from his fangs. The light dripped down on them, as long as the teeth of a grizzly.

Gresham had no way at all with women, but God had given him a way with dogs. He said very quietly: "Well, boy, do you think you've ever smelled this chunk of beef on the hoof before? Steady does it... Be easy, old son..."

He went on talking like that though Chris made a little jump, not away but toward him, and it seemed to Gresham that the green went out of those eyes and the mane fell and the teeth were no longer bared. He made sure, a moment later, that the big brute—only a Mackenzie River husky ever could grow to that poundage, surely—was actually sniffing at his bare hand.

That was when it came over him that he might have a chance to pacify the dog long enough to get to his revolver which hung from belt and holster against the wall. He was no man to try conclusions with that overgrown beast, Jarvis, but it was like Gresham to make a man-to-man fight of it if he could; and revolver against rifle would suit him well enough at close quarters.

HE TOOK a chance of losing his hand at the wrist by reaching out a bit and touching the muzzle of that big killer. Chris ducked his head back with a snaky fencing movement like one of those lightning feints which make a wolf entirely too fast for any dog; but an instant later the nose of Chris was sniffing at that same hand, and this time Gresham managed to touch the fur between the eyes. He felt the brute shudder under his fingertips. Yet what came out of the throat of the husky was not a growl but a whine, very soft—true dog conversation that astonished Gresham to the soul. He was so surprised that he spent an instant reaching for an explanation. Then he remembered that overgrown fluff of a puppy which he had sold to Jarvis. He remembered also the bad case of distemper through which he had nursed that youngster; and it was reasonably clear that Chris had not forgotten.

By that time his hand was petting the head of the dog and a whine was keeping that massive skull always in a slight tremor. Another moment and Gresham would have been up and reaching for his gun, but just then Jarvis came back with the lantern light swinging his huge shadow in waves and breakings of darkness across the wall. He carried a tarpaulin like a handkerchief with 100 pounds of stuff inside it. This he dumped on the table and fetched out something which he tossed aside.

"There's three days rations," he said. "You can fetch to the cabins up on Willow Creek with that chuck... The reason I gotta eat on you is my dogs got at my stuff and ate a week's grub in ten minutes... And besides, Alaska owes me something when I'm goin' out... Alaska oughta pay to get rid of me, eh?"

He began to laugh as he said this. His voice had a greasy bubbling in it, as though he had just been eating fish. It sounded like a seal barking. Then he was holding the lantern up head high and staring with immense eyes at a nightmare.

"Chris!" he shouted.

The husky bounded clear across the room to the door.

Jarvis came striding to the stool on which Gresham sat.

He roared at him: "What you done to that dog of mine?"

"I've talked to him," said Gresham. He studied the face of Jarvis. The man was in a sweat that could not be accounted for by the heat of the room.

"You lie," said Jarvis. "You lie, you got something in your hand. Leave me see what's in your hands!"

Gresham opened his empty palms.

"Nothing!" whispered Jarvis. Then his voice exploded through the room like a bomb. "You mean to say he remembers you? You stinking little half-breed runt, you mean he remembers you?"

There was six feet and a bit over of Gresham; at that he was a runt compared to this bit of Norse mythology.

A bit of silence followed this; the breathing of Jarvis made the

Jarvis lay flat on his back, huge feet sticking up in the snowshoes.

only noise. At last he said: "Call him. Call him and see will he come to anybody but me."

He stood back another long stride.

"Hai, Chris. Come here, boy," said Gresham.

That big fellow turned his head first, looked squarely at his master, and then sneaked across the room to Gresham. He put his head on Gresham's knee and closed his eyes under the hand that was laid on him. The heart of Gresham swelled with a novel emotion. He heard Jarvis muttering over and over again: "What's he gone and done to Chris?"

Then the big man broke into a roaring tantrum.

"You do without grub from here to Willow Creek!" he shouted, scooping up what he had left on the table and dropping it back in the tarpaulin. "You done something to Chris. I oughta take and pull the wishbone outa you. You Chris, you cursed fool...."

He took a mighty kick at the dog, but Chris was out of the cabin and into the night like a grey streak of lightning; and Jarvis rushed after him, still cursing.

It took Gresham a breath to come back to himself and the realization that he had been cleaned out of food. It was fifty miles to Willow Creek and in the Arctic night if a blizzard blew up while he was attempting the march....

Then something else startled him. He ran into the shed with the lantern and stretched out his hand toward the little buckskin sack that contained the gold. It was gone. It was more than gold. It was nearly two years of his life.

He ran back into the cabin, snatched out the revolver, and plunged into the open. The darkness was laid like a hand across his eyes, but he blundered on until he was deep in the trees. Then the cold knifed him down the back and brought him back to his senses.

He went back into the cabin. The opening of the door had allowed the outer air to fill the place with ice-water again.

He stood in the centre of the room for a moment, looking around at the blank walls which had framed those many months. They were empty, now. Because he had patted the head of a dog the fruit of his labor was snatched away from him. He looked down at his right hand curiously, as though the magic that had been in its touch might be visible.

FIFTY MILES of rough ground, snow, and a side-cutting wind is enough to kill most men, but it did not bother Gresham at all. He had read more than the books of '96, by this time; he knew something about the methods of that genius who has opened the doors of the Arctic wider than all other men, the great Stefansson. So he walked till he was tired and then lay down in the snow to sleep. Most mushers are afraid to do that. The legend is that the traveller who lies down must surely die in his sleep, but unless the brain of a man is drugged by exhaustion the cold will rouse him after fifteen or twenty minutes of repose that is almost more than food to the weary body. So Gresham slogged on and rested and slogged on again; and the aurora borealis grew up out of the dark to set the landscape trembling and light his way. When, actually, he reached Willow Creek, he told himself that he could have gone twice as far.

They had a good, big cabin up there that almost could be called a house. When he pushed open the door and stepped in, the heat, the taste of tobacco and the sweet fumes of tea in the air, made him a little dizzy. He made out the faces of the men one by one. There were half a dozen of them in the room taking their ease. They had the wherewithal to take it, too. There were even magazines; there was even a book or two. His mouth watered so that he could not speak at once. That was because of the smell of food and tea that was in the room.

A big man with a beard as blotchy as though it had been trimmed with a sheep-shears stood up and said; "It's that Gresham... What you want first? A drink or a smoke?... Jimmy, go and look out for his dogs before our mob gets the wind of them and tucks them away for supper."

"I didn't come up with dogs," said Gresham.

Nobody said anything to that, but they looked at one another a bit.

Gresham took a place over by the stove where he could face them all.

He said: "Jarvis stopped at my place with a gun. My two dogs are dead, now. And my dust is gone. I had thirty ounces. Jarvis took that. He killed my dogs; he cleaned me out of chuck; and he took my dust."

After this speech, he sat down on one of the bunks. Again, no one spoke. Then someone got out some jerked beef and somebody else began to mix a flapjack with flour, salt and lard. No one would look at Gresham.

At last the man with the chipped-off beard stood up and kicked at a burned match on the floor.

"All right," he said. "We gotta do something. We gotta do something."

Gresham always paid his way. He suggested: "I'll pay half the dust he stole."

Here the man of the beard looked across at him sharply, frowning.

"We won't be needing your dust, brother," he said coldly.

So Gresham knew that he had done something wrong again. He always was doing the wrong thing. Men were creatures of mysterious delicacies. For him it was easier to understand beasts like Jarvis, and Jarvis' dog. He looked down at his right hand and smiled faintly at it.

A moment later an uproar of dogs exploded near the house. When the door was flung open, Gresham saw just in front of it a snarling, worrying heap of huskies. That heap now burst apart, the savage dogs scattering off to the sides. From under them rose a grey monster with one dead husky laid at his feet. He looked after the retreat with a lolling, red laughter.

"Shoot that wolf! Hand me that gun," said the man nearest the door.

"Hai! Don't shoot!" shouted Gresham. "Hai! Hai! Chris!"

HE CALLED out, though his logical brain kept telling him that it was like summoning something out of a dream; the real Chris was far away with the team of his master. But now the dream materialized in actual fact, for the great brute that walked through the doorway was Chris beyond a doubt. He gave a green look out of his eye to the other men, right and left; then he went up to Gresham and sat down at his feet.

"He's killed that good dog. Tommy!" said a voice. "Look here, Gresham. I thought you said you didn't come up here with a dog?"

"Shut up, Barry," directed the man of the beard. "That's Jarvis' new leader. He leads Jarvis' team and he leads Jarvis. He's all the soul that Jarvis has… How come, Gresham? Could that brute Jarvis be on your trail here?"

The hand of Gresham was wandering idly over the head of the husky, and that strange, new emotion was wakening again in his heart as he answered: "No, he must have trailed me here. When he was a puppy, I sold him to Jarvis. That's all. He thinks he belongs to me." He found himself laughing. "Chris thinks he still belongs to me!" he explained.

"That makes you laugh, does it?" asked the man with the beard.

Everybody else was silent; they seemed to lean their silence like a shoulder behind the opinion of their chief. And Gresham knew that he was more of an outcast among his fellows than ever before. Yet he had not meant laughter at all. That had been to cover up something of unspeakable importance; something within him of which he was not exactly ashamed but which unnerved him.

Then he was eating a meal, while three of the men went out to harness a dog-team to a sled. He knew that he was making much trouble for them, and this filled him with shame. Thirty ounces of gold had seemed something infinitely worth while. The indifference of these people made it appear no more than thirty ounces of stone. It was plain that they were not setting forth to do justice on Jarvis so much because they wanted to get the gold back as because they wanted to see justice done; that impersonal and fleshless ghost which men call justice.

Once he put down his hand with a bit of bacon in it, the great teeth of the dog closed over bone and flesh, discovered its identity, then found and extracted the bacon by use of the tongue alone, delicately; an operation as precise as the threading of a needle.

After that he was out with the dogs and three other men and the long sled.

"Get on the sled," said the man with the black beard, whose name was Avery.

"I'll mush with the rest of you. I'm all right," said Gresham.

"Get on the sled, please," directed Avery. "We know that you're done in. Don't be a ruddy hero."

So Gresham got on the sled. "Do you know how to hit his trail?" he asked.

"If he's going 'out,' we can find him," said Avery.

So Gresham lay back on the sled, and as the dogs started up Chris ran beside him with a tireless lope. Gresham lay back and looked at the "merry dancers" in the sky. The aurora borealis was like a standing circle of tules with big heads of light and incredibly slight, trembling stems that seemed to bow and bend with the arch of the sky. After that he went to sleep.

HE WAKENED to the tune of a howling wolf. It proved to be Chris, who stubbornly remained off to one side though the sled was going on.

Gresham jumped off the sled, exclaiming: "Don't you understand? He's found the trail of his man. He's found Jarvis!"

Avery looked at him, said nothing, and then swung the team around. They headed in the direction of Chris. When they came closer, he started on ahead. At every small distance he was found waiting for them and then loping on ahead.

They kept that up for two days; and though snow often covered

the trail deep, Chris still detected it. He would plunge his head deep into the white smother, take a long whiff, and run on.

Gresham, who refused to ride the sled any longer in spite of fatigue, explained this to the others.

"He thinks he's going to bring about a happy reunion between me and Jarvis," he said, and he laughed.

They were silent.

"Because he's split up between Jarvis and me," explained

Jarvis kept his rifle pointed
at Gresham as the dog
leaped to the attack.

"What d'you want?"
asked Gresham.

Gresham, "he thinks that he's got to bring us together."

"Perhaps," said Avery dryly.

On the second day they found a sled loaded with bales of fine furs. There were silver fox that made the brain spin, guessing at values. There were mink and sable, too. Good sable, almost as dark as the best Russian quality.

"We're worrying him," pronounced Avery. "He's dropped his trail sled. He knows we're after him and he's dropped his trail sled. But it's a funny thing. There are only four of us. Knowing what Jarvis is, why doesn't he turn back and take a crack at us? What are four men to Jarvis?"

The third day they found a patch of trouble. The lead dog fell, biting at the bullet wound in his breast; and then the clang of a rifle flew out at them from a cloudy patch of trees.

In silence they cut the dead dog loose.

"If he can shoot like that with only the aurora to give him light," said Avery, "why didn't he shoot Chris, instead? He knows that Chris is the only reason we're able to hound him up the trail."

"Don't you see?" explained Gresham. "He's fond of Chris. He's too fond of him to shoot at him. Queer, isn't it? A beast like that, I mean. But he won't shoot Chris; and Chris is running him down."

Avery looked darkly at this explanation.

"How do you happen to know Jarvis so well?" he asked. "Ever a bunkie of his?"

"I don't know. I only guess," said Gresham weakly.

That was the day he suggested that they try Chris in place of the dead leader. They tried, and the thing worked perfectly so long as Gresham ran at the gee pole, singing out orders. But he had to stay there or else Chris turned into a devil and wanted to murder the lazy members of the team. So Gresham stayed, all of that march.

He did his share of the work when they put up camp, also. As he was working down into a sleeping bag for the night, Avery came and sat by him for a moment.

"Look," said Avery. "You're dead on your feet, but you're mushing farther and better than all the rest of us. What keeps you going?"

Gresham put out his hand, found the head of Chris, and worried it with his labor-hardened fingertips.

"Ever have dead years in your life? Ever want to bring them to life?" he asked.

"You mean the gold you worked for?" asked Avery. "You mean you want that back? Yes, of course."

"Well, there's the law, too," said Gresham uncertainly.

Avery pointed. "The dog doesn't play any part in it?" he asked.

Chris, jerking his head around, snarled at the pointing hand. Gresham took hold of the muzzle, absently. The big teeth closed on his fingers and gnawed at them softly.

"A dog?" said Gresham. "I thought we were talking about robbery and that sort of thing."

"I mean," said Avery, "that you're not wanting to wipe out the man who really owns that dog?"

"I?" gasped Gresham. "No!"

"All right," murmured Avery, and went away to his sleeping bag.

BUT GRESHAM lay awake for some time, thinking. Thirty ounces of gold meant over $1,000, which meant over twenty months of the medical school, which meant two years and a half. How could a dog enter among considerations of this importance? And yet the wise man, Avery, seemed to think that a husky dog was more important to him than the gold! There was no understanding among men. That was clear.

The next day they found various articles by the trail. Jarvis, hard-pressed, was lightening his main sled. He was making a sprint now for the mountains that loomed in the west, when the northern lights played in the sky.

They found queer things among his luggage. They found a *Robinson Crusoe* with grease-marked pages. "He knows how to read! Is he human, after all?" commented Avery.

Then they found some cooking utensils; even some beans and a sack of flour.

"He's going to live on his fat part of the way," said Avery.

Before the end of that march they got into the rise of land toward the mountains, and they found on the way the trail of a sled cutting deep in soft snow which still crumbled into the ruts. They could hardly be an hour behind their quarry. Then they came to a branch of an evergreen laid on the snow and on it buckskin sacks were piled.

"There's a thousand ounces here!" said Avery. "The man's going to have nothing but his naked soul with him before he leaves the country."

Gresham, staring at the little sacks, picked one up with an exclamation. It was his own gold. He held it in his arms, close to him.

"All right, then," said Avery, "you have your property. We can turn back, then, I suppose? The rest of us are ready to quit. We haven't more than enough grub to see us to the camp again."

Gresham threw his gold-sack aside.

"We'll get him tomorrow," he said. "When he tries to get up those slopes, that's where the strength of Chris will count double. Lighten the sled of everything we don't absolutely need for one day's march. We'll make a last stab at him. If we miss—then it's easy coasting all the way back; and we start home."

So they made that last day's effort with Gresham at the gee pole yelling orders, and Chris straining like a mad dog in his harness. They got so close that three times they saw the sled and string ahead of them and big Jarvis herding his dogs on. But they reached exhaustion without overtaking their quarry.

When they sat around the primus stove, Avery sat down beside Gresham with the curious eyes of a doctor making a diagnosis.

"You've had all you want, haven't you?" he asked. "We've made the last try, for you. Is it all right if we turn back tomorrow?"

"You've done all I asked," answered Gresham.

But his heart gave a hollow echo to those words, and a fear that had been in him all the way now became a conscious thing. He had known from the start, somehow, that he would have to meet Jarvis and fight it out with him for Chris. This use of numbers did not count. They had to square off man to man.

He took off a mitten and threw it away.

"Fetch it," he said.

Chris got up, slunk to the mitten, and brought it back. He sat before his new master and loved him with patiently enquiring eyes.

Avery said: "What do you want, man? A bill of sale? You have the dog, haven't you?"

Everyone was watching and listening. Gresham vaguely was aware of that as he answered: "It's this way—I haven't worked it out, but it's this way—he belongs to Jarvis. Jarvis is a beast who couldn't own anything, you may say. But Jarvis was fond of Chris. He taught Chris everything Chris knows. How to go and fetch that mitten, for instance."

"Well?" asked Avery, after an expectant pause.

"I don't know," said Gresham. "I'm going out by myself to think it over."

He took his revolver and went.

THE AURORA was in big arched bands across the sky; the shrubbery quivered, or seemed to quiver, with electric fire. Chris instantly took the trail, where the snow still was falling into the ruts. Gresham walked behind him.

But after a time he called the dog back to him. Chris came and stood before him with his head canted to one side, questioning.

"Look," said Gresham. "This Jarvis you want to bring me to so badly is no good. He's a rotten sort. You like me pretty well; you like him almost as well. But you're wrong. If you bring us together, there's only going to be a fight. Suppose you don't bring us together, are you going to keep hankering for him in your heart of hearts? Listen, is that what you're going to do?"

Chris, as though he wished to give the most patient consideration to this important question, sat down and waited for the next remark. It came from the rear, out of a patch of small, crowded trees, all leaning to one side from the prevailing winds.

It was the greasy voice of Jarvis, saying: "All right. I guess I got you now, Gresham... Chris, come here, you old fool!"

Chris neither stayed with his new master nor went to the old. Instead, he fled off to the side.

Jarvis, who had the butt of his rifle almost at his shoulder, still eyed Gresham.

He said: "I'd kind of like to linger it out. I've thrown away twenty years of work to get rid of you off my trail. And now I'd kind of like to linger it out a little. I'd like to get the taste of killing you all the way down the back of my tongue. Understand, you?"

"I understand," said Gresham, speaking without fear because, he felt, he was too tired to know anything but fatigue.

"What I'm wondering," said Jarvis, "is will he howl when you flop down in the snow? Will I have to drag him off howling because he wants to stay here with a dead man?"

"He'll want to stay here," answered Gresham.

"You got my gold," said Jarvis. "Why'd you keep coming after me, when you had that?"

Gresham looked at the face of the man, enchanted. The only light they had threw strange, trembling shadows that seemed to be a natural darkness of the skin. The thick-jowled face of Jarvis had grown wonderfully lean, with a pucker in the cheeks behind the corners of the mouth. After all, he had worked up the trail as one man against four, and with the four was the majestic power of Chris working against him all the time.

"I don't know why I came after you, but I'm here," said Gresham.

"Go for your gun," commanded Jarvis. "Go and fill your hand before I sock it into you."

"I'll go for my gun pretty soon," said Gresham.

"You wouldn't tell me," declared Jarvis, "but it kind of eats me, wanting to know what you did to him."

GRESHAM, LOOKING at him still with a curious calm,

wondered why the man still seemed superior to him, beast though Jarvis might be. Perhaps that was why it had been so frightfully important for him to meet Jarvis face to face.

"I'll tell you about it," said Gresham. "When he was a pup he was sick with distemper, and during his fever I used to set out cold water for him. I didn't know, but he loved me for it. That's the queer thing. He loved me for it. And I didn't know."

It was a word he seldom used, and it troubled him strangely.

"He's gunna forget you; he's gunna forget you!" shouted Jarvis.

"Take a mitten of mine after I'm dead," answered Gresham, with a strange surety, "and he'll think more of that than he'll ever think of you. Is there room in anybody to love two things at once?"

"You lie!" shouted Jarvis, and jammed the butt of the rifle against his shoulder.

That was when a shadow ran in behind him with a snarl. Gresham could not see whether the teeth of the dog actually touched his master or not, but Jarvis swerved suddenly, firing blindly into the air, and crying out in a terrible voice, "Chris!"

Gresham had his gun out by that time. He held it with both hands and fired. It seemed to him that he hardly had aimed it when Jarvis fell flat on his back.

He lay there with his huge feet sticking up in the snowshoes as Gresham went up and bent over him. The bullet had gone home through the left side of the body.

But that was not the important matter. The question was whether or not Chris had put his teeth into his old master. It would be simple to find out. It meant merely turning the body to one side; but somehow Gresham preferred to keep the question unanswered.

The shadow of the dog was falling across his feet and across the dead man.

He held out his left arm.

"Chris!" he commanded, and the big husky came instantly under his hand. Gresham dropped to his knees.

Then, without looking, using the sense of touch alone, he picked up handful after handful of the snow and scrubbed the muzzle of the dog. After that he stood up and walked slowly down the back trail. The others could salvage what was left of Jarvis' team and sled.

The dog, as soon as he understood the intention of the master, trotted quietly behind him, his nose never more than an inch behind the hand of Gresham.

Those softly following footfalls seemed to Gresham the only reality in this Northern world. The rest, and even his time of labor in the mine, was as dreamlike as the trembling of the aurora through the sky.

He began, as he walked, to dream of a Southern land where men labored little or not at all, where the sun gave to every soul a blessing greater than gold, and where the women were beautiful forever. He could hear their voices, and that imagined sound set him smiling, for they seemed to be hurrying toward him, laughing among themselves, and looking at him with eyes of eternal understanding.